Jerry raised Pepper, a cougar kit orphaned by a forest fire; the two became very close companions. But then the authorities intervene and demand that Pepper be caged. Jerry refuses to confine the mountain lion. Instead he will take her back to the area where she was born.

Jerry and Pepper run away. As they make their way deeper into the wilderness, Jerry tries in vain to teach Pepper to live off the land. Suddenly he finds their venture is going amiss; the two friends face real and terrifying danger!

Marian Rumsey's love and knowledge of the outdoors make her tale of a self-reliant boy and his unusual pet completely convincing in every detail.

LION ON THE RUN

LION ON THE RUN

by
Marian Rumsey

illustrated by Ted Lewin

**tempo
books**

GROSSET & DUNLAP, INC.
Publishers   New York

Tempo Books Edition
By Arrangement with William Morrow and Company, Inc.
ISBN: 0-448-05732-8

Tempo Books is registered in the U.S. Patent Office
Published simultaneously in Canada

Printed in the United States of America

For Marian, my namesake.

Contents

LION ON THE RUN

1 Pepper

"Don't become too attached to her," Father said, as he handed Jerry the tiny, towel-wrapped kit. "She's a mountain lion."

"Oh!" Jerry whispered, staring in wonder at the newborn baby whose ears were still flattened against her head and whose eyes were still tightly closed. "Is she mine?"

Father sighed. "For a few days." He had just returned home with the power-line crew and was tired and dis-

13

couraged. He was head lineman with the Challis Power Company and, for over a week, one of his assigned jobs had been to repair the electrical wires and replace the transformers damaged in the big fire in the Salmon River Mountains. "She was the only thing left up there alive," he said sadly. "One of the fire fighters asked if I'd take her until someone from the Wildlife Service could find a place for her."

"She's precious," said Mother, as she peeked into the folds of the kitten's makeshift blanket.

"She's a mountain lion," Father repeated insistently.

Jerry giggled at the helpless bit of fluff. "And fierce." He gently scratched the animal's chin and instantly the baby began to suck on his finger. "Oh, look! She's hungry."

"Sweet baby," cooed Mother.

"She's wild," said Father sternly. "It's not right to keep her. If she could have managed on her own I'd never have brought her home. You two don't realize. . . ."

"Oh, Father," Jerry said. "She doesn't even have any teeth!"

"She will soon enough." But in spite of himself he rubbed his finger over the polka-dotted kitten. "And for a while I suppose. . . ." He looked at Mother and then at Jerry and finally smiled helplessly. "She *is* cute."

But it was soon apparent that the problem of keeping

the baby might be permanently solved without further discussion. The kitten had not eaten for a long while and, in its weakened condition, began to slip into a state of semiconsciousness. To make matters worse, the veterinarian was in Boise and not due to return for two days. In desperation Father called their family doctor, and he offered advice on formula ingredients that they could try to feed to the kitten.

"I feel as if we've a baby in the house again," said Father, who had rushed back from the store with his purchase of bottles and nipples, milk and vitamins. Mother carefully prepared and heated the prescribed mixture and at last handed the bottle to Jerry.

"Oh, I don't want her to die," Jerry said, as he tried to entice the infant to eat.

Mother watched the baby weakly nuzzle the bottle. "With all this attention," she said, "she can't help but make it."

Jerry put the nipple between the baby's lips and let the warm milk dribble into her mouth. The tiny cat turned her head this way and that; then tentatively she began to eat. Within moments she was feeding greedily and noisily.

Father chuckled. "Well," he said cheerfully, while Mother and Jerry smiled rapturously, "it looks as if I've another mouth to feed."

Jerry found a small wooden box and moved it into his room, onto his desk beside his bed. He lavished constant love and attention on the kit; he listened day and night for her every whimper and cry. So when the kitten, who had known her own mother only a few days, finally opened her eyes for the first time, she saw Jerry as a perfectly fine substitute.

"Pepper," Jerry said later that week, smoothing her salt-and-pepper-colored coat. "I'm going to name her Pepper."

"I think Pudgy would be more suitable," Father commented dryly. "She's getting fat!"

Jerry grinned and rubbed the baby's tummy. She lay, feet in the air, on his bed beside Father, who had come up to his room to visit. Already the kitten had begun to pat at his moving fingers with her soft paws, and Jerry felt he had found a life-long friend. Now that her shiny blue eyes were open she was no longer content to remain in her box but loved to tumble onto his bed and bounce up and down on widely spread wobbly legs. Jerry stroked her back and played with her until finally she flopped down exhausted, sucking his finger in contentment.

"I hate to interrupt this cozy scene," said Mother, coming into the room. "But we have a visitor downstairs." Father glanced up at her inquisitively. She considered him for a long moment, then chewed at her lip pensively. "It's a park ranger," she said at last. "And he has a little wire cage with him."

Jerry gasped and clutched Pepper to his chest. She began to purr throatily. "No!"

"Oh, boy!" Father said grimly. "Now Jerry. . . ."

"No! I want to keep her!"

Father got up from the bed and shook his head. "I knew this was going to happen."

"But we can't very well give her up now," Mother said weakly. "I mean—she has all these feedings—her schedule. Jerry is up every four hours with her and—"

Father held up his hand. "It's better we let her go now."

"No!" Jerry said tearfully. "Oh, Father, please!"

"Perhaps we could just keep her until she's able to sleep all night without having to have her bottle," Mother suggested. "She's doing so well." She moved to stand beside Jerry and gripped his shoulder tightly.

Father glared at them both. "I can't resist you two," he said between his teeth. "I can't. But I'm right," he growled, "and you're both wrong. She's a wild animal, and she deserves to live like a wild animal and not be coddled like some lap cat."

"Please," Jerry whispered, but Father spun on his heel and quickly strode out the door. Mother bent to touch Pepper's soft coat. "Will—will he make me give her up?" Jerry asked, choking.

Mother smiled and shook her head. And she was right. Father turned to Jerry later that afternoon after the ranger left. "Well, she's yours. For as long as you want."

"Thank you," Jerry said with a rather unsteady breath. But Father's stern face kept him from saying anything more.

Within two weeks Pepper followed Jerry all over the house and was into everything. She squeezed under the sofa, chairs, cupboards, pillows, and rugs; she batted at everything that looked interesting, nibbled Father's shoe-laces with her new and sharp little teeth until he grumbled in irritation, and licked Mother's bare toes. She loved to run full tilt and skid along the slickly waxed floors, rolling over and over. She found the living-room curtains and lay on her back to box at them as they swung back and forth in the summer breeze. She discovered the tassels that dangled from the corners of the dining-room tablecloth and shook and tugged on them, until one day she succeeded in pulling the cloth completely off the table and over her head while the center-piece of frosted fruit tumbled to the floor with a crash. Pepper bolted through the room like a miniature ghost, with the whole family in hot pursuit. When Jerry finally caught her she spit and hissed, then cried and yowled for attention. Finally Jerry picked her up, cuddled her, and rubbed her chin until she purred happily.

"Don't you think it's time she discovered the front yard?" Mother asked, as she picked up the pieces of her favorite fruit dish. "Goodness, she's becoming a little terror."

Father kicked one of the kitten's squeaky toys into a corner. "Looks as if a cyclone went through here."

Jerry hastily carried Pepper out the door. Then he helped her down the front steps. However, the kit stopped stiff legged on the lawn and hissed viciously. "Don't be frightened," Jerry said soothingly, as she ran back to the security of his hands. "It's only grass." He moved her to the damp earth of Mother's flower bed, but she sniffed at it distrustfully and spit and hissed again. Suddenly a cement truck ground around the corner and roared down the street with a change of gears. Pepper leaped straight up in panic, turned, lunged blindly into the fence, then fell into the soft mud beside the garden hose. She staggered to her feet and howled piercingly.

"What happened!" Mother exclaimed, rushing out the door with Father.

Jerry held the terrified baby, whose tiny heart pounded furiously. "She's scared. There's so much noise."

"She surely does have a hair-raising shriek," Father said.

"But she was afraid," Jerry said protectively. "The truck—"

Mother shook her head. "Why don't you take her down by the creek? It's more peaceful there."

Father looked toward the house next door. "The Goodmans are going to wonder what all the racket is about over here."

Jerry bit his lip. Pepper was certainly not endearing herself to his parents today. He tucked the kitten under his arm, crossed the road, and started off through the open field toward the big trees and rocky hills. "You'll like it down by the stream," he told Pepper. "It's a special place." To the northwest for a hundred miles stretched the lonely mountains of Idaho's great primitive area. "It's where the wilderness begins."

In the protection of his arms Pepper soon stopped quivering and shaking from her fright and began to writhe and wriggle, ready to play. She chewed at his fingers and wrist and patted him with her paws. A grasshopper jumped up in front of them, and Pepper looked after it alertly with her cup-shaped ears at attention. Jerry stopped; he let her listen to it click away into the waist-high weeds that were crackle brown in the heat of the summer. A bird chirruped from the pines across the creek; the kit jerked her head toward the sound, then back as the grasshopper flicked off in another direction. "So much to see," Jerry said to her and stroked her fuzzy head. She turned and nibbled at his fingers and began to purr. "Silly baby," he said affectionately. "You don't even know what the world is all about."

In a few minutes they reached the stream, and Jerry stood on the rocky bank and looked at the trickle of water. It had been very hot and dry and it was lower than usual, but there was still a little green grass remaining in his favorite place. He kneeled once more and put the baby mountain lion on the ground. This time she was less nervous because Jerry was very still, and the peacefulness of the afternoon was soothing. Within minutes Pepper was nosing the grass, the stones, a slender willow branch. Soon she pranced through the weeds, boxed at each one that moved, sneaked between the stones, rolled in the dirt, and patted a small branch that jiggled just within reach.

Jerry tickled her nose with a dandelion puff and let her chew on a piece of bark. When she tumbled into the dirt exhausted, he went to the stream and soaked his handkerchief. He was gone only a minute, but she couldn't see him, and when he returned she was sitting in the middle of the clearing mewing pitifully. "What a crybaby," Jerry said and let her scramble into his lap.

"And you're a mess," he told her, as he began to wipe the damp cloth over her muddy coat. "Just look at you."

But Pepper purred so loudly that Jerry could hardly hear his own voice. She rolled her eyes in ecstasy. She loved to be washed and cleaned. Jerry giggled. "Now I know what it's like to be a mother mountain lion."

When she was more presentable, he put her in the grass where she lay on her back and played with a twig. She kicked it between her legs, bit it, and tossed it from one paw to the next. Jerry rolled away from her and lay on his stomach in the shade of a thick cover of brush. She was entertaining to watch, and as long as she could see him she was perfectly content to be alone. In a few minutes Pepper sprawled over on her side and yawned, and Jerry knew she was ready to take a nap in the warm sun.

He closed his own eyes for a moment. It was a sleepy day. He breathed in the sweetness of the dried haylike weeds. He heard the muffled mutter of the creek as it murmured along. He wondered idly what Mother was going to have for supper. It was getting on toward that time of day. He would have to feed Pepper first, though. If he didn't she would never stay in her box until he finished his own meal. He opened his eyes and looked at the little cat. She was sound asleep, yet he knew in another few minutes she would be off again and into all sorts of mischief. A shadow flicked over the grass just in front of him, then was gone.

Jerry considered the day when Pepper would sleep through the entire night. It would surely be cause for a celebration. It was a good thing he was on summer holiday or otherwise Mother and Father would never let him get up at odd hours during the night to feed her. Again that shadow blinked briefly between him and Pepper.

Father had suggested that Jerry start the kit on some solid food, and Mother had suspected baby cereal would be best. Jerry thought for a bit about the complicated problem of teaching Pepper to eat from a dish. Then he frowned. Whatever was that odd shadow that kept reappearing on the grass? He shifted uneasily. Something kept crossing the sun's path, yet he couldn't see what it was because of the bramble under which he was lying. But he had no more time to worry over it, because there was a sudden rustle, a heavy beating. Jerry rolled into the clearing with a start. He sat up, and his eyes widened.

A great red-tailed hawk was dropping to earth right in front of him. Its huge wings were pulled back to slow its speed, its claws were distended, and it was heading right for Pepper. Jerry gasped and flung himself forward. "Go away!" he yelled. The bird swerved violently. It had not expected Jerry, invisible from aloft, to erupt out of the thick stand of brush. At the same moment some instinct warned Pepper of danger. She leaped to her feet and raced headlong for the nearest scrub. The hawk banked and hurtled toward her. Jerry threw up his arms, shouted, and lunged at the bird. Again it shied, touched the ground with one claw, wheeled, raked Pepper across the back with the other claw, clutched, then lifted her into the air.

Jerry gasped in horror. He threw handfuls of dirt and rocks and forced the hawk to dodge to one side. It was frightened of Jerry, yet determined not to release its catch. Pepper fought with every ounce of her strength. She squirmed like an eel. Jerry screamed. The bird reeled, off balance, and with only a shaky grip on the kitten was forced to drop her or flounder to the dirt before Jerry's pummeling. Then with its prize lost, the hawk winged upward with a rush. In seconds it was over the tree and disappeared from sight.

"Pepper!" Jerry sobbed. The fall to the ground must have killed her. He thrashed through the thicket. He tore apart the brush. Finally he found her. She was crouched in the deepest shade. Her hair bristled and stood straight out, and she spit and hissed ferociously. Jerry closed his eyes in relief. She hadn't been hurt after all, for the hawk had been unable to get a firm grip. And he ought to have known that when a cat takes a tumble it always lands on its feet.

*   *   *

"She was extremely lucky," Father said, when Jerry rushed home with Pepper in his arms. "You were out of sight and dead quiet. The kitten is very tiny and appeared to be alone and unprotected." He sighed. "You must understand, Jerry, that you are dealing with a wild animal, and that a kit is natural prey for a bird like a hawk. You must take better care of her," he said sternly, "while she is still defenseless."

2 Growing Up

But Pepper did not stay small and defenseless much longer. Jerry succeeded in teaching her to eat from a bowl. At first she was a messy eater. She stepped in her dish, pushed her face into the food, and always managed to coat herself from head to foot with cereal. After each feeding Jerry was forced to clean her thoroughly with a wet cloth. But eventually she began to eat with more dignity, and in a few weeks he was able to add strained baby meat and eggs to her gruellike meals. With this added nourishment she seemed to grow in great leaps and bounds, and by the time she was five weeks old she slept through the night for the first time. It was a good thing. School had started.

And then, in another few weeks, she was forced into giving up her bottle entirely. Mother was the one who induced this momentous event. Since Jerry was in class, she was now required to feed Pepper during the day and very soon informed him that she had much more to do around the house than to cuddle and bottle feed a spoiled kitten. Pepper was thoroughly upset by this high-handed treatment, and she responded by causing a period of upheaval around the house. Forever underfoot, she constantly wailed for someone to pick her up, pet her, scratch her chin, or even feel softhearted enough to produce her bottle and give it back. She disliked being separated from Jerry. He never tired of her company. He was always ready to play. Quite soon she learned to identify the sound of the returning school bus and met him at the door with yowls and purrs of pleasure.

One day, when the cat was three months old, Mother faced Jerry with a problem. "You have to do something about this animal." She pointed at Pepper, who was busily engaged in chasing her black-ringed tail and bumping into the furniture with loud crashes and thumps.

"When you aren't home, she is into everything. It's time she stayed outside by herself. She is just too big to be in the house all day long."

Jerry tossed his books on the table, caught Pepper, then tickled her nose with her tail tip playfully. She was taller than his knees now and quite strong and sturdy. "I know she would never be attacked by a hawk again," he said. "She's too large for that. But I wouldn't want her to run off. There're so many cars. She might get run over."

"I bought her a present today," Mother said.

"A collar!" Jerry was pleased. It was bright red leather, and he quickly buckled it around Pepper's neck. She promptly ducked her head right and left, trying to see what was there. Then she sat down, scratched at it, and attempted to reach it with her long, raspy tongue. "You look very handsome," Jerry told her and distracted her momentarily by tweeking her ear. Instantly the cat flopped on her side ready to play with him, but as she did, she tipped over the magazine rack and sent the contents slithering over the floor. She was up like a flash, the collar forgotten and accepted, and skidded over the slick pages and ripped and shredded them as they riffled under her nose. Jerry pulled her aside and began to pick up the mess.

"I also bought this," Mother said carefully.

Jerry sucked in his breath. "A chain!"

guess we're stuck with her now," he said with a chuckle. He put his arm around Jerry's shoulder. "But it looks as if you're going to have to do something in order to preserve the peace," he said. "Come on out back and let's see how we can keep a cougar from becoming a pain in the neck."

The next day a large load of wood and wire arrived from the lumberyard, and when Jerry came home from school he examined it thoughtfully. It had been decided that Jerry must build up the backyard's low wire fence. If Pepper was to be left outside without being chained, it would have to be at least six feet high so she could not leap over it. But after the first ten minutes of work Jerry realized the job was going to be long, tedious, and require lots of hard work. He went to the telephone and began calling his best friends to see if they would help.

"Are they coming over?" Mother asked, as he shambled back through the kitchen after a few minutes.

Jerry shook his head.

Mother sighed. "Too bad. I'm not much for digging post holes, but I'll make you some lemonade, and I did bake cookies today. I'll bring them out later." She smiled at him as he hung onto the back screen and tickled Pepper with the toe of his boot. "What's the matter?" she asked.

"They *can't* come over," Jerry said.

Mother shrugged. "Well, they're ten, too, and fifth grade does mean more homework."

Jerry put his arms around Pepper and squeezed her tightly. "It's not that," he said, as the cat began to purr loudly. "It's their parents. They say that Pepper—" Jerry looked at Mother unhappily. "Their parents said Pepper might bite."

"Good heavens!" gasped Mother. "Has she ever nipped any of your friends?"

"Of course not!" Jerry said angrily. "She wouldn't hurt a flea."

Mother sighed. "She *is* getting awfully big."

Jerry nodded. "Can you imagine what she'll be like when she's full grown!"

Mother shuddered. "I can imagine what the *house* will be like." She laughed and pushed him out the door. "Quickly! Start building your fence!"

Jerry smiled broadly. "Won't she be magnificent?"

Father was the one who helped him. He worked with Jerry when he came home each afternoon, and in a few days they enclosed the yard snugly. When Pepper took her first run, Jerry was pleased to see she seemed very happy. She galloped around the fence's perimeter and examined the wire carefully. Then she nosed into everything, stopped long enough to sharpen her claws on the pine that grew in the middle of the yard, then began to root in the garden.

"There go my fall flowers," said Mother with resignation. Pepper scratched at the soil, scattering it every which way.

"It's just as well," Jerry said shrewdly. "They make Father sneeze."

Next Jerry had to build Pepper a house. Jerry said that he could not manage the job, but Father quelled him with one of his fierce looks and informed him that it was high time he learned to use tools.

One whole evening was devoted to drawing up the plans. It took them ages to agree on what ought to be included. Mother wanted the house to have a raised floor, so Pepper need not sleep on the cold ground in winter. Father insisted mountain lions slept on the earth in their natural dens and that she was spoiling Pepper beyond reason. Jerry soothed them both by drawing in a wooden floor for half the house but leaving the other side bare. Then Mother wanted the house to have a flat roof, so Pepper could satisfy her urge to climb by scrambling onto its top. Father said a flat roof would collect puddles of rainwater and be hard to keep free of leaks. Jerry drew in a peaked roof, but he added a front porch that was flat so the cat could survey her domain from its height. Mother finally said she would like the finished product painted white to match the main house. Father insisted that the color would show the dirt and always look messy. Jerry made them agree to paint the sides white but the roof dark brown.

"But does it have to be so big?" Jerry asked in dismay. Putting such an assemblage together seemed a nearly impossible task.

"When that kitten grows up," Father said, "she is going to be a giant." He called to Pepper, who was stretched out comfortably on the sofa. She looked up lazily and yawned, displaying a mouth full of teeth. Father sighed and went to her, saying, "Apparently she's too fat to move." He stretched the tape measure down the length of her back. "She's almost two feet long now." He ran it from her paws up to her spine. "Nearly a foot and a half tall. And she must weigh ten or fifteen pounds."

"Fourteen," Jerry corrected. He had spent a difficult few minutes last week getting her on the bathroom scale, and her weight was all too clear in his mind.

"She'll be ten times that when she's grown," Father said. "This shelter cannot possibly be any smaller." He scratched Pepper's chin. She flicked her tail tip slightly and began to purr so loudly Jerry and Mother heard her on the other side of the room.

Jerry studied the plans spread out before him. "I don't

know if I can build this or not," he said for the ump-
teenth time, but when he saw Father huff up in prepara-
tion for a lecture he went on hastily, "but I'll try!"

He started next day. The first thing he did was to tack
the plans to the side of the house, since Pepper's new
outdoor home was to be built nearby. The cat took one
look at the crinkling paper that fluttered intriguingly in
the wind and swiped it off the wall with a well-aimed
bat.

"Stop that!" Jerry yelled, as she began to box with it.
"For crying out loud," he said angrily, wrestling with
her in the grass. "Let go! You're ripping the paper."

Ten minutes later he had the drawings retaped to the
wall. By now they looked as if he had used them to build
twenty houses. They were wrinkled and rumpled and
held together with Scotch tape. The instant they were
firmly in place, Pepper ran to pull them down. Jerry
tugged her away, then dragged her into the kitchen.

"I don't want her in here," Mother said. "I'm frosting
a cake. It's difficult enough making these twirly pink
roses without her underfoot."

Jerry grimaced and took the cat back outside. "Sometimes, cat, you're a pain," he told her. He snapped the
leash to her collar, then tied the other end to one of the
posts that supported the porch railing. She began to yowl

unhappily and paced restlessly back and forth. Even before Jerry could decide what he had to do first in his construction job, she was fighting her chain fiercely. She boxed, pulled, hissed, and tugged. Finally she squatted on her hind legs and reared backwards with all her strength. The collar choked her. She gagged and coughed, and Jerry ran to set her free. But he was not fast enough. The post to which she was tied suddenly broke with a pistol-shot crack, and the sudden release sent Pepper somersaulting.

"What on earth was that!" Mother exclaimed and pushed open the door. Pepper bolted past her legs. The piece of porch post that trailed from her leash terrified her. She ran full speed through the kitchen, bumped the table as she passed, and knocked the cake Mother had been frosting onto the floor. Jerry ran after her, kicked the coffee table, and accidently upset it. He slipped on the hall rug Pepper had sent skating into a wad and fell with a crash into the hatstand and sent it toppling.

Pepper lunged up the stairs. The piece of wood clattered noisily behind her, and she bounded blindly into the bedroom. When Jerry finally caught up, she was beneath Mother's and Father's bed. He climbed under beside her and soothed her until she stopped trembling and shaking. Then he unsnapped the hateful chain. In a few minutes he wished he could remain under the bed forever, for he heard the brisk click-click of Mother's heels as she came up the stairs determined to rout them both out.

"I didn't have a very good day," he said grimly, when Father came out back after he arrived home from work.

"Umm," was his answer, and he stood, arms folded, staring at the clumsily patched porch.

Jerry started on the house again the next day, and very soon he realized what a truly spoiled kitten Pepper was. One of his first chores was going to be to teach her not to tear everything that was lying around loose into bits and pieces or carry them off between her front paws like downed prey. At first he tried giving her a swift swat with a rolled newspaper when she used her claws to scratch at something important or began to chew on the tools he laid out to use. But this method had no effect whatever—she soon decided the paper was a toy and shredded it into confetti.

Jerry dragged one of the sixteen-foot planks between the sawhorses he had brought from the garage for his work, and with a piece of white chalk carefully marked the board into two eight-foot lengths. He turned around to get the saw, and as he did Pepper trotted up and neatly licked off his mark with her moist tongue so he had to make it all over again. Finally he flexed the saw ready to begin the cut. However, she was fascinated by the movement of his hand and began to chew at his wrist.

"Yow!" he yelped. "Stop that." There was no getting around it. He had to do something about her mischief making. She was only playing, but he had work to do. And she was liable to be cut by the sharp tools lying about. Jerry considered the problem. He didn't want to hurt her; he could never whip her or do anything cruel. But at last he had a brainstorm. He dashed into the house, up to his room, and rummaged through his locker full of toys. When he had what he wanted, he rushed back downstairs to the kitchen where Mother was scrubbing potatoes and squirmed in to reach the faucet.

"I thought you were building a lion house," she said, raising one eyebrow at him slightly. "What are you doing playing with water pistols?"

Jerry filled four plastic guns. "I'm going to teach Pepper some manners," he said grinning wickedly.

"Now," he told the playful cat outside, "you had better mind me. From now on when I say no, I mean *no!*" Once more he went back to work. Once more Pepper loped over and began to watch the saw blade as it glistened in the sun. The moment she raised her paw to cuff at it, Jerry shouted, "No!" She ignored him as usual and boxed the saw. "No!" he said again and shot her squarely in the face with a squirt of ice-cold water.

Pepper leaped straight up, spat, and ran toward the kitchen, where she clawed at the screen, demanding to be let inside. Jerry stalked up the steps and stood over her. "No!" he said sharply, for she was not supposed to rip at the screen. But she continued to scratch and paw at the door. "No!" he repeated, and when she refused to mind, he shot her full in the face again. She bolted across the yard and dove under the hedge out of sight. Jerry smiled to himself. Pepper hated water more than anything on earth.

He went back to his sawing, for if he didn't get on with it Father would be home and he would have nothing to show for another afternoon's work. At the same time Pepper peeked out from under the bushes. "You may come and watch if you behave yourself," he told her. "But one false move—" he shook the water pistol in her direction "—and you'll get it!" Pepper slunk back into the brush.

Jerry ran the saw over the mark on the plank and made his first messy start. It was difficult to hold the blade straight, for his arm wobbled and shook, but once he got into the meat of the wood the work was a little easier. Before long the sawdust began to fly. In five minutes the board was in two pieces, and they dropped neatly to the ground in front of him. "Gee," he said in a pleased voice. "That's pretty good."

Pepper squirmed toward him on her belly, and he walked over and patted her on the head. "I still love you," he said, then picked up another board to saw. He laid it between the sawhorses, made the mark, and began his cut. This time his start wasn't so ragged, and he had the sixteen-foot plank in two pieces in less time. He slid the sawhorses closer together, then laid one of his last eight-foot lengths in place.

Pepper came up and nosed his elbow, then rubbed back and forth against his legs and purred. Jerry measured and marked the plank with the chalk. Pepper reached out her long neck, sweeping her tongue over the white line swiftly. Jerry picked up the squirt gun. "No!" he ordered.

The cat flicked the tip of her tail and laid back her ears. Very, very slowly she inched toward the chalk mark again. Her eyes were slitted as she looked at him defiantly, and her lips were drawn back to expose her sharp milk teeth. "You better not," Jerry said, laughing under his breath. She swiped her tongue over the board lightning fast, but just as quickly Jerry shouted "No!" and squirted her fiercely. She snarled and ran for the porch and the back door, but Jerry knew what she was going to do and followed hot on her heels. She saw him com-

ing and made one lightning slash at the screen in hopes
Mother would let her in. Then Jerry shouted and shot
with the squirt gun again. She yowled and fled for the
cover of the hedge. Jerry sighed and went back to work.

Within minutes he had the planks out in a rectangular
shape. "Hey, Pep," he called, "come over here and see if
you'll fit." But she was not about to come out of hiding.
Jerry walked to the wall and examined his plans. This
construction project was something like building a model
from a kit only on a grander scale. He found the tape
measure, searched through the wood stacked beside the
fence, and located the necessary boards. By now he was
beginning to saw fairly straight, and the next few sec-
tions were cut neatly and quickly.

Back again he went to his plans for another check,
scratching his head thoughtfully. He had to assemble
his planks, which was not especially easy to do. But at
last one corner appeared ready, and Jerry sorted through
the tool box for the bag of nails and the hammer. With
the first pound he knocked the whole lot to one side, and
he was forced to readjust and straighten all over again.
His next nail bent over like an accordion, and he had a
fearsome time getting it out. He realigned his boards
and started another time. By now he was hot and sweat-
ing. He ran his hand over his damp forehead and glared
at the framework in front of him. Nailing was just as

hard as sawing. But he was determined to pound the nails straight or die in the process. It took him over an hour to get the four corners hammered into place, and he did so by sheer perserverance. He strode up to the kitchen door and called Mother. She came out with Pepper. She had told Jerry earlier that he was being mean to such an adorable kitten by getting her all wet with the water pistol, and to Pepper's relief Mother had let her inside.

"Look what I've done," Jerry said smugly.

She examined his work thoughtfully. "What is it?"

"It's a mud sill!" he stormed.

"Oh. Well, it looks very nice for a mud sill."

Jerry sighed. "It's the base for her whole house," he explained.

"When are you going to start the walls?" She twitched the ties of her apron away from Pepper, who had begun to box at them.

Jerry smiled. "Right now!" He dragged an immense eight-by-four panel of plywood off the pile of lumber and held it up against one side of the sill. "Would you like to watch? I'm getting pretty good at driving nails."

But Mother was trying to retrieve her apron strings from Pepper's claws. "Let go," she told the kitten. "You're tearing the material." Pepper rolled over in the grass and nearly pulled Mother down with her. "Ooof!" she gasped. "Jerry, give me your squirt gun!"

Jerry giggled. "I thought you said I was being mean to her."

"Water," Mother said firmly, "never hurt anyone." She aimed at Pepper, then tugged at her apron. "No!" she said fiercely to Pepper, but the cat continued to pull playfully. Mother squeezed the trigger and blasted Pepper with a well-aimed stream of water. The kitten leaped to her feet, ran for the back door, looked back at Jerry as he shouted, made no attempt to claw the screen in her usual manner, but shot off to hide beneath the hedge. "How about that," said Mother, as she pocketed the water pistol in case of future need. "I do believe Pepper is learning to be a lady."

When Father came home, Jerry had the two side walls nailed into place. He also had laid another eight-by-four panel across the sawhorses and drawn a line down the center. The huge slab had to be cut into a pair of four-foot squares for the end walls.

"How am I doing?" Jerry asked, as Father thoroughly examined his work.

Father nodded. Then he looked carefully at the sheet of plywood Jerry was preparing to attack with the saw. "You must cut the door in one of those pieces," he said. "Be sure and follow the plans exactly, for the opening has to be three feet square. She will need all of that when she grows up." He called to Pepper, and she ran out from under her hedge retreat to receive a friendly scratch on the chin. "How about a before-dinner snack?" he asked her. "I hear you've been having a bad day."

"Hey!" Jerry called. Father poked his head back out the kitchen door. "Aren't you going to help me?"

"What forever for?" he asked. "But I'll be sure and call you when supper's ready."

Jerry muttered and went back to work.

It took him three full days, working after school until dark, to make that one long cut and shape the door. When he finished he was so sick of sawing he wanted to scream. His morale didn't improve when his best friend came by the second day on his bike and asked him to go down to the field to play ball. Pepper trotted up as they talked through the fence.

"She surely is getting huge," Steve said, as Pepper stood on her hind legs and licked at his face with her raspy tongue.

"She's over three months old," Jerry told him.

Steve scratched Pepper behind her chin through the wire. "I wish she belonged to me. You're lucky, Jerry." Then he looked at the pile of lumber, the tools, the mess of woodworking dust that lay beside the sawhorses. "My dad won't ever let me build anything," he said enviously.

"I certainly wish you could help," Jerry said. "This sawing takes forever."

"Sometimes my folks are really weird," said Steve. "Pepper is about as vicious as a soggy squash."

Jerry sighed. "I know, and she's learning to mind some." He patted his holstered water pistol. "I've started training her not to be a big pest." He went back to sawing the plywood. "Have a good game," he said between strokes.

"Yeah," said Steve with a grimace. "I guess. I'd much rather help build a lion house."

Jerry grinned as his friend pedaled off, and he stopped long enough to tweek Pepper's tail. She turned and boxed at him, then ran for the big pine and zoomed up it to the first branch. Sitting in the crotch, she gave herself a good wash. In a few minutes she inched out on the limb until she was directly over Jerry. Still as a mouse she watched him work. Her fat bushy tail hung down over Jerry's head. He jumped up and cuffed it playfully. "Yeah," he said. "I guess I am kind of lucky at that."

Eventually he managed to get the four walls nailed into place, then four corner posts to reinforce the whole structure. But when it came time to put on the roof he needed help, for it was too heavy and complicated for him alone. So Father came to supervise and, to Jerry's disgust, make him redo nearly half of what he had spent the afternoon working on. Jerry grumbled unhappily at the added chore.

"You certainly don't want it to lean precariously," Father said with a shrug. "My advice is to do things correctly the first time after this." But at last Jerry adjusted the roofing at the proper angle, and Mother came to watch as he nailed it firmly into place.

"Wow!" he exclaimed, as he stepped back to admire the finished product. "Look at that." Pepper zipped in and out the door of her new home. "Oh, she loves it!" Jerry said. On hands and knees Jerry crept inside the shelter with Pepper. "It's nice in here," he shouted. "I can use this for a clubhouse."

"I'll make her a nice rug," Mother said and bent double to peek in at them. "So she won't get cold."

"Coddled cat!" Father grumbled.

Jerry slithered back outside. "See, it's even got eaves." He pointed them out to Mother proudly. "And how about this porch!"

"You must paint it," Mother reminded him.

"But that'll be fun."

"White, remember."

"And a dark brown roof for me," Father said, grinning.

But Jerry left the inside just as it was, for he thought Pepper would like the fresh woody smell. He had to put two coats of paint on the outside, but when everything was dry Jerry's very last job of all was to letter *Pepper* painstakingly over her door. "I'm done," he marveled.

He danced around foolishly and made wild swipes in the sky with his brush. "I'm done! I'm done! I'm done!"

That night Mother made a special celebration dinner with a coconut cream pie, and for the occasion Pepper had a large dish of milk and Friskies.

"I truly didn't think I could build it," Jerry said later and to no one in particular.

Father looked up. "Don't you know a person can do almost anything if he tries hard enough."

Mother smiled at Pepper. The kitten was lying on the sofa beside her and had her head on Mother's lap. "I hope you enjoy your first night in your new home," she said to her.

Jerry gaped at Mother. "Night!" he blurted. "But she's not going to stay out there at night!"

"Oh, but—"

"She sleeps on the foot of my bed," Jerry said. "She doesn't want to sleep out there all by herself in the dark. That house is just for days!"

"Talk about big babies," Father said dryly.

"Besides," Jerry added, "she's four months old today, and she's learned how to be a good girl." But when Father and Mother looked at him long-faced he amended that statement with a grin. "That is—" he patted his holstered squirt gun "—as long as I'm nearby and armed to the teeth."

3   Pepper in Trouble

When Pepper was six months old she began to lose the spots of her first coat. She was growing up. Her chubbiness disappeared, and her body became leaner and longer, yet her legs remained strong and sturdy. Her paws suddenly seemed too large for the rest of her, her ears oversized, her tail too lengthy. Her teeth at a half a year were quite fearsome, and the whole family was pleased that she was sufficiently trained to refrain from chewing on anything except one of Father's worn-out lineman's boots.

Her claws, too, were formidable. She kept them tucked out of sight nearly all the time, for she was still terrified of her dreaded enemy, the water pistol, that continued to be aimed at her on occasion. She had put the old pine in the back yard in bad shape. She loved to sit before its rugged trunk and sharpen her claws on it into razor-sharp blades. Father had wrapped the tree's base with heavy Manila line so it could bear her attacks, but it never lasted very long. Pepper always ripped it to pieces.

Yet she loved the pine. She could never seem to satisfy her urge to climb, and if she was not lounging sprawled across the porch or snug and asleep in her house, she was usually up that tree. Jerry had great fun as he tried to spot her in the thick foliage. Usually he sighted her tail first. For though Pepper was very shrewd about hiding, she always forgot about her tail. Invariably it hung down and gave her away. One of her favorite napping places was on the heavy overhanging limb. She would straddle it while her four legs and tail dangled down limply.

She had begun to greet Jerry with a new warbling, whistlelike sound though most of her talking still resembled that of an ordinary house cat, only louder and more intense. She continued to sleep most of the night on Jerry's bed, though lately she had begun to annoy Father with her nocturnal wanderings about the house. Pepper loved to play with shadows and rustled about just enough to rouse Father, who was a light sleeper. Jerry knew the time was coming when she would be forced to remain outside. But that would not be so bad. Spring was just around the corner, and he could take his sleeping bag to her house and stay with her until she adjusted.

Yet as much as Pepper liked the backyard, it did not give her sufficient area for the exercise she really needed. Father told Jerry if Pepper had been living in the wild she might have had a range territory of up to thirty miles, and she would have kept in trim as she constantly moved about searching for food. Jerry had to admit that Pepper was a trifle overweight. So as soon as the weather cleared up and the snow melted, he began to take her for long walks. Then one crisp, clear Saturday he gave his bike its spring overhaul. Since Pepper had grown so much these last few months it had become nearly impossible to keep up with her on foot. She had boundless energy and could outdistance him a hundredfold, and yet she needed her gallop every day to keep fit.

He wheeled the bike out of the garage. Today he was going to try something new. He collected the kitten, who was asleep on the sofa, and snapped the leash into her collar. She disliked being chained and pawed at it for a moment, then tolerated the hateful lead because the prospect of a walk pleased her. "I know you don't like it," Jerry told her with a friendly pat. "But it's a necessity until we're away from people and houses." He took her outside and wrapped the end of the chain around the handlebars of his bicycle.

"The idea," he told her, "is for you to be a good girl and just come along beside me as I ride the bike." He got on and rolled down the drive. Pepper eyed the spokes as they sparkled in the sun and followed him happily, cocking her head at the wheels with interest. As soon as Jerry began to pedal she danced beside him and cuffed at his moving feet. She promptly tangled herself in the leash and forced Jerry to stop and unsnarl the kinks. But before long she trotted beside him perfectly content. If she enjoyed one thing best, it was to get away from the house and go out into the wide world.

Jerry rode slowly at first and let her become used to his riding. When they were a few blocks from home he gave her more lead, and she was able to range farther from his pedals. He began to pick up speed, and Pepper loped beside him, bubbling with enthusiasm. They turned the corner and headed north on the unused back road that paralleled the endless stand of pines. Soon they had left Challis, not a very large town, behind them. Then

Jerry pulled up, unsnapped Pepper's chain, and let her run free. The moment he did the cat reared on her hind legs and boxed at the air in sheer pleasure.

In a moment Pepper turned from him and ran full speed along the road's edge. Jerry pedaled furiously to catch up. Yet when he began to close the gap between them she lunged off at a tangent and into the thick brush. In seconds she reappeared fifty feet farther up the road and galloped back toward him. When it looked as if she would run over him, she swerved and leaped the culvert of the opposite roadside in a graceful stretch. But now she was back again, boxed playfully at his bicycle wheel as she side-stepped past, then dashed full speed into the thicket. Jerry giggled. She was so happy that she nearly exploded. He pedaled on, and in a moment she pranced up beside him. It was a wonderful day for Jerry. They went for miles.

When they eventually turned back it was after lunchtime, and even later when Jerry stopped at the main road. There he should have leashed Pepper. He sighed. She was having so much fun and did not want to go home. Jerry stroked her head and listened to her rumbling purr. The urge to show her off was irresistible. It would only be a few blocks out of their way to detour down by the park. He knew Steve was probably there playing ball.

"Come along," Jerry said and pedaled toward the

field. "In fact," he told the kitten, as she loped along not far away, "there's Steve now." He shouted and waved. Recognizing his buddy was easy because of his bright red hair. But the moment Steve saw him Jerry's mind registered three important facts. Steve had his dog with him, the park seemed to be crowded with people, and he had not chained Pepper.

Steve's dog was a big Labrador named Rex, and he always had been a good friend. As he caught sight of Jerry he ran down the street to greet him with a tail-wagging welcome. But in a moment the dog saw Pepper and changed instantly into a black, bristling, baying beast. Rex liked to chase cats, and it mattered not one bit that Pepper was just as large as he was. Jerry lunged for Pepper's collar, for he knew there was going to be trouble. But he missed her and nearly ran over Rex, who suddenly darted in front of him. Jerry put on the brakes violently, skidded across the sidewalk, and crashed straight into Steve. Both of them clattered down in a heap.

Jerry untangled himself from the wheels and handle-bars, and rushed after Pepper. "Stop!" he shouted. But the kitten had never seen a dog at such close quarters, and she was terrified of the deafening noise the animal made as it followed hot on her heels. She streaked across the grass, through a collection of adults who had spread out a picnic lunch. With startled shouts and screams of "Mountain lion!" they scattered.

Jerry ran as hard as he could after her, passing a frightened-looking woman who hurried toward the safety of her automobile parked nearby. "Pepper! Pepper, stop!"

"Rex!" Steve shrieked, as he sprinted up behind Jerry. "Come here!"

But neither Pepper nor Rex paid any attention. Rex was in full voice and was determined to catch the flash of lightning that had bolted directly across his path. Pepper, frightened out of her wits, heard nothing but the dog's growls and threats and deep roaring bellows, and she instinctively sought safety by climbing out of his reach. She chose one of the spotlight standards that were used to illuminate the night ball games.

"Oh, no!" Jerry moaned and threw himself at the pole as he tried to stop her. But she was too fast. Her claws dug into the wood, and she climbed beyond his reach.

"Jeepers," Steve gasped, as he snatched Rex's collar and began to beat his dog into silence. "Jerry, she'll fall!"

"Pepper," Jerry shouted. "Pepper, stop!" But the kitten went higher and higher with great clawing lunges. They watched horrified until eventually she reached one of the bracketed spotlights almost at the top. For a breathless moment she slipped on its slick surface and was forced to claw frantically at the wooden pole to save herself. This seemed to frighten her more than ever, and she went even higher.

"Oh, make her stop," Steve pleaded. But Jerry could only watch the kitten helplessly until, at last, either completely exhausted or feeling that she was finally in a place of safety, Pepper halted of her own accord. "It's miles up there," Steve said, frightened, "Make her come down!"

Jerry's heart pounded. "I don't think she can," he whispered. "If it was a tree, she could. But she'll fall from that barren pole." His blood ran cold at the danger Pepper was in. "She's up so far."

"What'll we do?" Steve groaned.

Jerry gritted his teeth. "Father. I must get Father! Wait here," he said over his shoulder, as he began to run up the street. "There's a phone at the filling station."

"I won't leave her," Steve said. "Hurry, though. Oh, hurry!"

But Jerry was told that Father was out on a job, and at this heart-sinking news he nearly burst into tears right then and there. "I—I need him," Jerry choked to Father's supervisor, and he quickly explained what had happened. He hated to do so. Father detested being called from his work for some family problem, but Jerry felt this emergency was an exception. "You must find him," he said over the phone. "You must!" The supervisor was very kind and told Jerry that he would put out a call on the radio right away. He was sure the truck could be located without too much difficulty, since the crew was installing transformers at the new housing development on the far side of town. That satisfied Jerry. Father would come if he received the message. He rushed anxiously back to the field fearful that Pepper might have fallen. But she was still atop the standard. She had braced herself between the wooden pole and one of the spotlights. The picnickers had reappeared and, with their hands shading their eyes, were watching the cat anxiously.

"Is he coming?" Steve asked tensely.

Jerry nodded; he was breathless from his run back. "They put out a radio call for him. If he's near the company truck, and he hears it, he'll come."

Steve wiped his hand across his mouth nervously. "Jerry, if she tries to come down—"

"I know." Jerry shivered. "She'll fall."

"I hope he gets the message quickly," Steve muttered. "I hope he hurries."

A man in a red jacket came up to them. "Hey, kid," he said to Jerry sharply. "That *is* a mountain lion up there, isn't it?" he jerked his thumb toward the top of the pole.

"Yes, sir," Jerry said quietly. "She belongs to me."

The man shook his head suspiciously. "We thought for sure that beast was going to start ripping us apart."

"Oh, no!" Jerry gasped. "She's just a kitten!"

"My dog was chasing her," Steve explained. "She was running from him."

"She won't hurt anyone," Jerry said shocked, then turned to a woman who approached them from the crowd.

"I told you it was a wildcat," the man said to her. "Belongs to this kid."

"Well, what on earth is it doing in town?" she asked nervously. "Letting it run around loose like that endangers lives."

Jerry shook his head helplessly. "No," he whispered. "Pepper would never hurt anyone."

The man turned away from him impatiently. "Come away from the pole, Jennifer. Kitten and tame or not, I certainly don't want to take any chances if it does come down."

Jerry turned to Steve as the couple walked back to the rest of the group that stood beside their automobiles. "Father's going to skin me," he said wretchedly. "I'm not supposed to call him at work. And I'm not even supposed to let Pepper off the chain in town."

"I didn't think Rex would take off after her like that," Steve apologized. "She's so big now."

Jerry nodded. "I forgot how much he likes to chase cats. Suddenly the crowd gasped, and Jerry sucked in his breath. High overhead Pepper had moved ever so slightly. Small splinters of wood blew off and away. "Oh, don't try to come down," Jerry breathed helplessly. "Pepper, don't try it."

"It's miles up there," Steve said shakily.

Jerry fought back tears. "It's a hundred and twenty-five feet." A long time ago Father had pointed out this fact as they waited in the stands for a night game to begin. Father could take one look at a pole and nearly always tell its height exactly. Jerry gulped. "It's one of the tall ones."

They waited forty-five minutes, and to Jerry it seemed an eternity. He had never seen the kitten look so helpless, and never had he felt so inadequate and useless. He wished desperately that the growing group of people keeping the vigil with them would go home. Jerry did not like their comments and suggestions or their insinuations that Pepper might attack them like a vicious animal. They didn't seem to pity her helpless plight at all.

But at last Steve clutched his jacket. "Look!" The orange-colored power company truck had just rounded the corner.

They ran to meet it, and Jerry wrenched open the door before the truck had rolled to a complete stop. "Father!"

"I know," he said tensely. "I see her."

"It was my fault, Mr. Parker," Steve said, nearly in tears. "Rex chased her."

Jerry gritted his teeth. "No," he said firmly, "it was mine. Pepper wasn't chained."

"Well, it doesn't much matter one way or another now," Father said grimly, and shaded his eyes to look up at the kitten.

His partner, Frank Murphy, came up to stand beside him. "Boy, she's really up there!"

Father shook his head. "That's no place for her to be."

Jerry followed them to the back of the truck, which was filled with tools, terminals, and transformers, and what seemed to be a million miles of reeled wire. Father picked up his climbing rig, and Mr. Murphy began to fold a large net bag made of strong, lightweight Dacron.

Father sighed. "She's going to be a handful. She's frightened." He slipped his safety belt around his waist; then he slung a coil of line over his shoulder. Mr. Murphy handed him the net, and he put it in the canvas bucket hanging from his lineman's belt. As they walked to the base of the pole Father turned to Steve. "I'd appreciate it if you would take Rex home," he said. "Pepper will be pretty hard to handle if the dog should bark as I get up there."

"Yes, sir," Steve said, and he shot a last miserable and apologetic glance at Jerry. Quickly he ran his dog down the street toward his house. Father kneeled and began to strap on his climbing hooks—the bucket crane on the truck was far too short to reach as high as he must go for Pepper. When he had them firmly buckled he turned to Jerry. "You seem to have gathered quite a crowd," he said coldly. "And they do not seem especially happy about seeing Pepper on the loose." Jerry was miserable. "Now. Do not call to her or speak," Father ordered sternly. "If she hears your voice she might try to come down. Do you understand?"

Jerry nodded and watched as Father placed the safety strap around the pole, then snapped it into his climbing belt. He went up about four feet, stopped, leaned back, adjusted it to a better position, and tested the spikes on his feet. Mr. Murphy led Jerry out from under the pole. "Might as well stand over here," he said. "That way we won't have to look into the sun." Jerry knew that Mr. Murphy really wanted him out of the way so he wouldn't get hurt in case Pepper fell. Jerry gripped his stomach with both arms. He was frightened and felt sick.

"Don't worry," Mr. Murphy said gently. "Your dad will get the cat down all right. He's done more than one rescue operation in his time." But Jerry had not been thinking of Pepper just then. His thoughts had been on Father, who had to go up that slender pole. Mr. Murphy sighed. "I guess you know he wasn't very happy about having that call come from the main office."

Jerry shut his eyes briefly. He was all too aware of

Father's feelings, and he knew what Mother was going to say, too. If Father skinned him, Mother would hang his skin out to dry on the back fence. He looked up at Father, who by now was over halfway up. At that moment Pepper suddenly readjusted her position in order to look at him as he made his ascent.

Mr. Murphy moved beside Jerry uneasily. "I hope that animal doesn't decide to come down right in your dad's face."

Again Pepper moved ever so slightly. She clasped her two front paws around one of the huge spotlights. "The current!" Jerry gasped. "If the bulb breaks—"

"Power's off," Mr. Murphy said. "We had that taken care of right away."

Pepper squirmed another time, her back foot slipped, and for a moment she seemed to be suspended in space. She snatched frantically at the wooden pole, then hooked onto it tightly.

Father was almost up. Jerry knew that he was talking to Pepper, for, far below, they clearly heard her shrill, terrified yowl as she answered him. Jerry could hardly swallow. Up there on that pole were two of the three lives that were more dear to him than anything in the whole world. One was supported by two steel spikes and a thin leather strap; the other clung precariously with razor-sharp claws. Jerry clenched his fists, and his nails dug into his palms as he watched Father take the net out of the canvas bucket. The cold spring wind was blowing briskly up there, and the thin mesh blew out and billowed slightly. Pepper jerked away. Then she left the slight protection of the lamp shield and clawed her way upward.

"Oh, no!" Jerry whispered. But in a moment the kitten was forced to stop. Her head was now even with the very top of the pole, and she hugged the wood and cried pitifully. Her long tail hung down and flicked back and forth. It touched Father's yellow tin hat and whisked across his face as he inched upward. He was talking to her, soothing her, calming her. But if she should move again, and should start to fall, there was nothing left for her to catch hold of, except, perhaps, Father. Jerry stifled a sob.

Once more Father took out the net, then carefully re-adjusted his weight and dug in his climbing hooks firmly. Very slowly he slipped the meshlike bag around Pepper's hindquarters and up over her back. Even from so great a distance Jerry could tell the kitten did not like the feel of the material in her unstable and risky position. She moved the barest inch. Bit by bit Father raised the net. He reached across her back and drew it around her shoulders. From such a distance the cat looked nearly as large as Father and almost as heavy.

Suddenly Father jerked the bag right over Pepper's head and straight down over her face as far as her front legs that clutched the pole. The next instant he struck the kitten in the side with his fist. The pain must have been unbearable, for Pepper released her hold ever so slightly and lurched sideways away from him. As she moved Father hit her again, and this time Pepper let go completely. Jerry cried out, and he gripped Mr. Murphy's arm in horror. There was a blur of movement overhead. Father had either slipped or had dropped down a few feet intentionally, and the pole shook and swayed. There was a screaming roar from Pepper as she clawed desperately to keep herself from falling, but she was hindered by the Dacron mesh.

Then the net bag closed with a violent jerk, and she was safely encased in a tight ball. But Father, now forced to take the full strain of her weight, was flung against the pole with a cruel crash. Mr. Murphy stiffened; the crowd gasped. The next instant Father pushed back from the standard and readjusted his position and Pepper's. His partner let out his breath in relief, shoved Jerry aside, and ran to the pole. Father, using the coil of line he had taken aloft, had begun to lower Pepper to the ground like so much dunnage. A minute later the kitten arrived unhurt in Mr. Murphy's competent hands. He snapped her leash into her collar, then began the task of releasing the cat, who was ensnared in the mesh like a tangled fish.

But Jerry was not concerned about Pepper just then. She was alive; that was all that mattered. Father, however, was still aloft. He needed much longer to come down the 125 feet than had Pepper. At last he put his feet on the ground, and Jerry was there to meet him.

"I'm glad she didn't weigh any more than fifty pounds," Father said, as he unbuckled his safety belt. "Is she okay? I had to hit her pretty hard to make her let go."

Jerry nodded. "I thought—I thought—" He gulped back tears.

Father looked at him grimly. "That I'd let Pepper fall? You didn't have to be afraid of that."

Jerry stepped back and faced him fiercely. "Oh, Father! I was afraid for *you*!"

For a long moment Father stared at him. "Jerry—"

"I know!" Jerry said hurriedly. "You don't have to tell me! I'll never let her off the lead in town. Never, never, never!"

Father sighed tiredly. "How many many times have I tried to make you understand that Pepper is basically a wild animal. In times of stress or danger she is going to follow her natural instincts. Today she climbed to escape from an enemy that was nothing more than Steve's dog." Jerry bit his lip miserably. "Do you realize that in the wild she never would have gotten into trouble like this? If she had climbed, she would have climbed a tree, and eventually she could have come down herself. That electrical pole is more of an enemy to Pepper than Rex ever will be."

Jerry nodded unhappily. "I understand that."

Father shook his head. "I wanted to give Pepper up when she was a kit, because I knew something like this was bound to happen. Taming Pepper has made her completely dependent upon you, Jerry." He flung his hand toward the pole. "I hope you understand clearly that if she had tried to come down just now she would have been killed."

Again Jerry nodded miserably. Then, behind them, one of the crowd spoke. "I knew that animal was going to hurt someone. It ought to be kept in a cage. Just look what it's done to that lineman."

Jerry sucked in his breath. "Oh, your arm!"

Father turned to look at his bloodsoaked sleeve. He heaved another heavy sigh. "It's just a scratch," he said to the woman. Then he turned to Jerry. "But I could have used the squirt gun. For a minute there Pepper did forget her manners."

Jerry's tears came then. He flung himself against Father as if he would never let go. But Mr. Murphy had untangled Pepper from the net and had been waiting patiently.for Father's lecture to run its course. Now he handed him Pepper's lead.

Father put the chain into Jerry's hand. "She belongs to you, Jerry," he said gravely. "See that you take better care of her."

4 The Ultimatum

Father did not mention that terrible day again, but it had
so frightened Jerry that he became doubly cautious. He
not only never let Pepper off the lead near town, but he
never again took her for her runs near electric poles.
She had suffered no physical injury at the ball park, but
the experience had left her terrified of dogs. In the following months when she ran free, meeting them was un-
avoidable, yet if she was frightened and climbed from

them, Jerry made sure that she only went up a tree. And this did happen on occasion, despite the fact that by the time Pepper was two years old she was by far bigger and outweighed any dog with the courage to chase her.

On the first day of his Easter vacation, however, Jerry's world suddenly began to fall apart. He was in the back-yard hammock reading a book, a present received on his twelfth birthday a few days before. Pepper was playing nearby with her newest toy, a car's old rubber tire. She dragged it about the yard, leaping and attacking it with snarls and playful cuffs. Even though she was two years old, Pepper still remained kittenish in her ways.

"Jerry, come inside, will you please?"

Jerry dropped the book instantly and sat up startled. He thought Father had left for work already—it was late. He frowned and followed him to the living room, then tensed. Mother was there, too. She sat on the footstool, her hands clenched together nervously. Jerry swallowed. Whatever had he done?

Father sat down in his chair. Then to Jerry's surprise he handed him a long slim envelope. "Here."

Jerry slipped out the official-looking letter and read it. At first he could not clearly comprehend what it meant, but as he read it through the second time he felt an icy clutch of horror. "I—I don't understand," he whispered.

Father rubbed his fingers across his eyes. "It means we have notification from the City Council and the City Zoning Department that we cannot keep a mature non-domesticated animal." He kept on rubbing his eyes tiredly. "We have to get rid of Pepper."

Jerry's stomach clenched into a knot. "No," he breathed.

"We've half expected something like this," said Mother. "We knew about the ordinance and assumed it would be only a matter of time before it was enforced because Pepper is an adult now. We've talked about it, or tried to, but you've never wanted to listen."

"I hate this town!" Jerry exclaimed, as his face contorted with emotion. "I hate every living inch of it!"

Father sighed sadly. "Perhaps you do at this moment but not deep down in your heart."

"Pepper wouldn't hurt anyone," Jerry said. "They have no right to say she's dangerous, or a killer, or a threat to the community."

"She's a mountain lion," Father stated softly.

"She's my friend!" Jerry shouted. "And I thought she was yours and Mother's, too!"

"Oh, Jerry, don't," Mother said miserably. "You know we love that silly beast just as much as you do. But she's grown up now, and to anyone that doesn't know her she has all the appearance of being vicious. And you must be fair. Sometimes wild animals in captivity do revert to their natural instincts." She took a long, unsteady breath. "And you must remember the time over a year ago when Rex chased her up that light pole at the park. She truly got into dangerous trouble then, and those people that saw her were more than a little upset." She shook her head sadly. "And she was just a kitten when that happened."

Father stood up and began to pace restlessly back and forth across the room. "Jerry, you must face the fact that Judge Bailey has given us notice to find a place for her outside the city limits."

Mother put her hands to her lips, and Jerry knew she was on the verge of tears. "We put off telling you all this until the last minute," she said unhappily, "because we knew how badly you would feel."

Father sank back into his chair, and it groaned beneath him. "The moment the sheriff gave us this warning I tried to get a transfer into the back country," he explained. "But there weren't any openings. After that Mother and I set to work to try to find someone who would give her a home. Sheriff Anderson and Judge Bailey have been helping us, because they realize how much Pepper means to our family."

"You mean you didn't just get that letter today?" Jerry whispered.

"It came last Monday."

"Last Monday!"

"It's not easy trying to find a person willing to take a full-grown mountain lion," Mother said softly. "She's not an animal most people want as a house pet."

"I won't give her up!" Jerry said bitterly. "Even if you found her a home, I won't give her up to some stranger!"

Father shot a quick glance at Mother. "Well, you needn't worry on that account," he said shortly, "because we simply could not find anyone who wanted to take her anyway."

Mother continued seriously. "But we have come up with a solution, and we've been waiting until we were absolutely certain before we broke the news. Father wrote to your Uncle Frank, and he called us last night. He said that he would be happy to come and take Pepper, and he's arriving today. Pine Hills is lovely country, and you know Uncle Frank loves animals very much."

Jerry's heart plunged. "But—but that's over three hundred miles away!"

Mother nodded sadly. "I know, but we'll try to make the trip as often as we can."

Jerry licked his lips. "And what about Old Muddy? Pepper is afraid of dogs," he said helplessly.

"Oh, now," Father said brusquely, "a great big moose

like Pepper can't possibly be afraid of a little hound the size of Old Muddy. The only real problem I can see for Frank is the cost of buying her food. That cat eats like a moose, too. But we'll find some way to manage that."

"But she *is* scared of dogs," Jerry insisted. "They terrify her. You know that!"

Father thumped his hand hard against the mantel. "There's one more thing you must know, Jerry. You'll not like it either, but you'll have to accept it. Uncle Frank will have to cage Pepper."

"Oh, no!"

"Frank works in town. He can't let her roam, and it's dangerous to leave her chained."

"But she'll die if she's caged," Jerry whispered. "Oh, please, don't let Uncle Frank pen her up."

"There is no other way," Father said unhappily. "I don't like it either, but there simply is nothing else left for us to do."

Jerry stared at Father helplessly. "We—we—" He swallowed, then went on unsteadily. "We could take her into the mountains. We could let her go free."

Father put his hand on Jerry's shoulder and shook his head. "You know we've been very careful about not letting her stalk anything but butterflies and grasshoppers, which has left her without the slightest idea of how to kill her own food. All her life Pepper has eaten meat-market chopped hamburger. If it isn't mixed with Friskies and put in front of her every evening, she lies there and wails like a baby. Now face up. You know she probably could never manage on her own. You can't want her to suffer the horrors of starvation."

Jerry gritted his teeth. "But I don't want her caged! If she can't live with me, at least I want to be able to see her every day and take her out for walks." He choked back tears. "There must be someone who'll take her near town."

"Yes," Father said and took another deep breath, "there is one other place. When Judge Bailey realized we couldn't find a home for her, he called the city zoo and practically begged them into accepting her. They contacted Mother while I was at work yesterday. Pepper would have to go through nearly a month of quarantine, but after that—"

"The zoo!" Jerry gasped in dismay.

"Well, it *is* a place," said Mother, "and except for Uncle Frank's it is the only other home we've been able to find."

"There is always one final way, Jerry," Father said grimly. "But since Pepper truly belongs to you that would be a decision you would have to make yourself."

"You mean—have her put to sleep?"

Father nodded. "Perhaps in the long run it might be

fairer to Pepper. I don't like the idea of penning her even in Pine Hills and with Uncle Frank, who I know would take the world's best care of her. It's against nature to imprison a wild thing. We were dead wrong to have kept Pepper when she was a kitten. I knew this moment had to come."

Jerry could not stand any more. He turned and ran from the living room, through the kitchen where the warm smell of baking bread met him with a sweetness that he did not want just then. He burst out the back door, leaped off the porch, and ran to Pepper's house. She raised her tawny tan form from the grass at the sound of his approach and sat back on her powerful haunches as Jerry flung his arms around her sleek neck and let the tears come at last. For a moment Pepper opened her mouth slightly and exposed glistening razor-sharp teeth. Then she twitched the tip of her long tail and swiped her tongue across Jerry's damp cheek and, from the depths of her chest, began to rumble her deep purr of pleasure.

At last Jerry leaned back against the wall of Pepper's house and wiped his hand across his eyes. Oh, how he would miss her. He thought he must surely die of heartache. Such a blow, and without warning, was almost impossible to bear. Absently he began to stroke Pepper's head, which she had rested across his knee, and in a moment found her favorite scratching place just behind

her chin. Her eyes closed to narrowed slits of ecstasy as she absorbed the touch of his hand. How much she had grown from that tiny kit Father had first handed him! Now she was six feet long, stood twenty-four inches high, and weighed nearly one hundred and twenty-five pounds. Her salt-and-pepper-colored spots of babyhood had disapeared long ago, leaving a smooth brown coat that rippled and shone on a powerful body. Her underparts had become the creamy white of the adult mountain lion, and the black streak over each eye and the moustache marks on either side of her nose made her lower nose and mouth appear startlingly white.

It was unbelievable that she would be gone from his life so soon. Uncle Frank would bring his truck to take her to Pine Hills, and they would put her in a cage for the long ride. Jerry bit his lip and once more fought back the tears. He looked at the mountains that loomed all around. They were hazy in the warm spring morning. Over there on the middle ridge was where Father had found her, just a mewing helpless bundle. He stirred restlessly. Pepper moved slightly and cocked her head, helping him relocate her scratching spot more quickly. Father could be wrong; Pepper might be able to fend for herself in that country where she had been born. And spring was a good time.

Jerry got to his feet. He had been sitting with Pepper

for hours, long after Father had finally gone to work and Mother had driven downtown to shop. It had rained the night before, and Mother never liked the house tracked with Pepper's gigantic muddy prints, but Jerry felt she wouldn't really mind today. Pepper would be gone soon enough.

He opened the back door, and Pepper loped in ahead. After a quick scratch at the closed cupboard door where her Friskies were stored, she bounded into the living room and onto the sofa, where she poised on the over-stuffed seat with all four feet nearly touching. Jerry flopped down beside her, still lost in thoughts of her caged forever. He wished Uncle Frank would never come, although he sincerely appreciated how Uncle Frank had leaped at the chance to keep Pepper when no one else would. He sighed and watched the big cat as she methodically licked the telephone that sat on the end table. It jingled slightly and was beginning to get drippy. He tugged at her collar and pulled her away.

Perhaps Uncle Frank's old truck might break down. It wasn't in very good shape at the best of times. Then he would be able to have Pepper with him just a little longer. He felt almost too miserable to breathe. Next he began to worry that his uncle might bring along his dog. Old Muddy was a nice-enough hound, but with the scent of a mountain lion close he would set up a howl that would turn Pepper into a bundle of nerves in seconds.

Jerry got back to his feet and began to prowl the room aimlessly. There must be some better place for Pepper. There must! What could he do? Pepper hit a magazine with one giant paw and sent it skating off the table. She was after it in a second and batted it playfully right and left like a hockey player moving a puck. She crashed into the coffee table, tipped it over, and Father's pipe tobacco spilled into a brown heap on the rug. Jerry frowned at the unsightly mess, but then he heard the bookcase teeter as Pepper backed into it. She pushed her nose against the Chinese dinner gong, and it bonged gloomily as it rocked on its ebony legs.

"Pepper, stop that," Jerry said softly. At that very moment his horribly tilted world shifted back onto its axis. He had decided what he must do about Pepper. "Shame on you!" He gripped Pepper by the tail and dragged her along behind him as he stood the coffee table back on its feet and straightened the bookcase. He scooped up the tobacco in his hand, poured it back into the container, and slammed on the lid.

Jerry began to really hurry now. He ran upstairs while Pepper loped along beside him. He pulled his backpack out of the closet, his bedroll, and cook pans . . . down the stairs again and into the kitchen, where he stuffed as much food as he could into the pack's front pouch. He ran to the freezer on the back porch and pulled out a rock-hard parcel, which he put into a small wicker clothes basket. He raced back into the living room, found a piece of paper and a pencil, and wrote a scribbled note. He read it through once very carefully, for it was important that Father and Mother clearly understand this written plea. In it he explained how badly he wanted to save Pepper from enduring a lifetime of misery, and how he planned to work out a solution to Pepper's problem on his own. He felt sure they would be sympathetic; they would give him the opportunity to try his luck. He signed it, then propped the note on the mantel where they would be sure to see it.

"Stop it!" he shouted at Pepper, as she began to sharpen her claws on Father's chair. He tugged her away, only to have her box playfully at the fireplace tongs and scatter ashes everywhere. Quickly Jerry dragged her outside. His bicycle leaned against the front steps, and he hooked the clothes basket onto the rear rack and tied the bedroll on top. He threw the camp pans into the front basket with a clatter and slipped the pack onto his back. Two minutes later he slammed the front gate and shot a glance over his shoulder.

Pepper was standing in the middle of the flower garden, boxing Mother's daffodils every which way as she tried to reach a black-and-gold butterfly that kept jerking just out of her reach. She looked so foolish that Jerry couldn't help laughing. "Come along, Pepper," he called.

The mountain lion looked up, realized Jerry was pedaling off without her, and in one beautiful, graceful leap cleared the front fence and bolted after him like a golden flash.

"Silly cat," Jerry said affectionately and snapped on her leash until they were out of town. He grinned at her. "Do you know where you're going?" he asked, as she bobbed along beside him like a hobby horse. But he didn't expect a reply so waved his hand at the distant blue-gray mountains. He was taking her to a special place where the whole family sometimes packed in to camp in the mountain wilderness of Idaho's great primitive area. It was there that Pepper must make her home. Jerry knew the place was not far from where she had been born, and this seemed very important. But it was a long way, and the thought made Jerry shift up and send his bicycle surging ahead with a double burst of speed.

He had to give Pepper this one chance. If she could not find her place in the big hills, then her life would be over. Jerry could never let her live out her days, frightened, cramped, and lonely, in a cage with a howling hound housed beside her.

5 Leaving Home

Their troubles began before the day was out. Jerry, traveling fast, was quickly approaching the turnoff by the airport. At that point he left the usual route to the family's favorite campsite. He had to make the trip in the longest way possible, by fire roads and out-of-the-way trails, and most of it on foot, for he needed time in which to teach Pepper how to hunt.

Jerry looked over his shoulder. Pepper was hanging

back since she had discovered that the day's trek involved much more than her usual romp. She was still a trifle overweight, slightly out of condition, and she was thirsty. Spittle dribbled from her lips, and Jerry knew she wanted to lie down under a shady tree and rest.

Nevertheless, they left the deserted paved highway and bumped off into the secondary road that led toward towering Twin Peaks. At first the road was relatively smooth, but by midafternoon, after all sign of habitation had vanished, the grading deteriorated into ruts and rocks. Jerry leaped and lurched on his bike. At last he pulled over under a stand of thick pines and parked. He dug out his camp kit, found the largest pan, and filled it with water from his canteen.

"Come on, girl," he said, as Pepper caught up. She drank greedily, then flopped down in the shade. A bird trilled somewhere in the trees, but she was not even interested enough to look up. Jerry sat down beside her and began to pull stickers from her whiskers. She twitched her nose and chewed at his fingers, and he pulled at her long canine teeth playfully. But she was too hot and tired to do even that for long, and she yawned at him. Jerry began to scratch her chin and let her rest.

By now Uncle Frank probably had arrived from Pine Hills, and the resultant uproar caused by Jerry's and

Pepper's absence must be awkward to say the least. He could visualize the three of them arguing over Jerry's actions. Father would be pretty sure his effort to take Pepper into the mountains to live on her own was totally useless and the inconvenience he was causing Uncle Frank nearly unforgivable. Mother would worry that he would get lost or struck by lightning or fall into a pit or get a case of poison oak.

Uncle Frank, however, would be the intermediary for him. He was like Father in many ways, and he would understand. Uncle Frank would remind his parents that Jerry was twelve now and knew his way around in the mountains, and he would be the one to persuade them to let Jerry try in his own way to help Pepper. Jerry ran his hand over his eyes. Reluctantly, in the back of his mind, he saw the reason for the City Council's demand that Pepper be removed from the city limits. The family always looked on Pepper's foolishness as a hilarious joke, but Jerry was not blind to her dangerous potential.

"Time to go," he told her and gave her tail a mighty yank. It was immensely long, heavy, and thick. Jerry stood up and whacked the dust from his pants and pushed his bicycle back to the fire road. He wouldn't be able to take it much farther; he was due to start into the deep wilderness shortly.

"Oh, do come on," he said to Pepper over his shoulder. She had roused herself at last and was now creeping through the grass low to the ground in her hunting crouch. Her shoulders were two butting humps, her head was dipped forward on a tensely tightened neck, and her tail rippled only the barest fraction. She had drawn back her black lips over her viciously sharp teeth, her ears were laid back flat against her head, and along the ridge of her back the hair prickled and stood out. Jerry grimaced. Pepper was stalking a green-backed caterpillar beetle, and, if she was up to her usual mark, it was going to get clean away. For a moment Jerry felt a tremor of anxiety. Would she ever be able to hunt? he wondered.

His original plan had been to camp in a place where his scout troop sometimes trekked for their overnight camp-outs, but with all his stops to wait for Pepper as she investigated everything that moved, the sun sank long before he was there. He and Pepper actually could have made it easily enough, but the fact was that he didn't much care for the darkness that had descended over them. He pulled up again, waiting for Pepper to appear. When she did bound up to him she rubbed against his leg and purred throatily. Somewhere in the far distance an engine chuffed, probably at one of the logging camps on Loon Creek. But there was nothing else, except the swish-swish of Pepper's tail tip as she flicked it back and forth across the pine needles that lay thickly underfoot.

Jerry knew she was keen-eyed and alert; nights were Pepper's time. Still, he wasn't very sure of the way ahead. Without a moon it was dark as pitch. He had been along this route a few times but never at night. He snapped Pepper's chain into her collar, and she began to make soft little yowls of discontent and to pace restlessly to the end of her lead. Jerry looped one end over his arm and pushed the bicycle along the uneven fire road. He couldn't risk riding in the thick darkness with so many unseen ruts with Pepper threatening to throw him off balance as she tried to chase every little noise. To top everything, Jerry was starving and wanted his meal, but the only place left for them to stop and make a decent camp was farther ahead, beside the creek. It was very near one of the logging camps, and there were a couple of houses nearby, too. That didn't please him especially, but he had no choice since it was getting so late.

The fire road climbed steadily, and before long fog settled. The trees dripped down on them like rain, and the sound the water made in the underbrush as it pattered somewhere out of sight was more than a little disturbing. There was no denying—Jerry was miserable. He didn't like the thick mists around his immediate world. Although he knew that the mountain was just punched into a cloud, the scrub and pine around him still seemed monsterlike in the dark gloom. The rattle of his bicycle over the uneven ground seemed overloud, and the donkey engine, closer now, sounded as if it were coming from some dismal underwater cavern. His bike was getting heavier by the minute, and one pedal occasionally clipped his shin painfully.

Pepper, too, was no help. Strong as a team of horses she forever pulled and tugged to be free, yet he dared not let her go. Most likely there were dogs in the two houses somewhere up ahead. If she heard them bark she might run off in a dead fright and climb a tree.

Within the hour they came to the ford at Loon Creek, and Jerry stopped to look at it thoughtfully. The water gushed and bubbled around the rock barricade that had been built over the top of a pair of very old pipes. The pipes served as a culvert, letting the creek through the somewhat solid half bridge. As usual, however, the rusty pipes must have been clogged with brush or stones, for they were not carrying off all the water. The stream gurgled over the top ledge, so that even the highest part of the crossing was underwater. Jerry looked at it with a touch of distaste. Normally to ford the little creek was fun, and he usually ended up not only wading across, but building dams, sailing bark boats, skipping stones, or trying to catch the polliwogs that lived in the marshy eddies. But crossing the foot-deep ford with his friends in the middle of a warm afternoon was a lot different from doing so at night with a loaded bicycle and a reluctant mountain lion in tow.

However, there seemed to be no choice, since the place in which he wished to camp was on the other side of the creek. He sighed and sat down on a rotten tree stump to take off his boots. Pepper came up and licked at his toes. "Oooh!" he gasped giggling, and shoved her away. "That tickles." On his feet again he winced at the sharpness of the rocks. He took another turn around his wrist with Pepper's chain, tossed his boots in the basket, then pushed the bicycle into the water. It was cold as icicles, and he danced around on his toes. The stones were slippery, and unable to see where he was stepping he teetered this way and that.

He had passed the halfway point when the chain suddenly tightened. Jerry stopped, looked over his shoulder into the mist, and saw Pepper still on the dry bank. Obviously she hadn't been beside him as he thought. He had been more concerned about his tender feet and keeping the bicycle upright than remembering that she would doubtless object to putting her warm paws in the rushing ice water. She was sitting down on her haunches in her all-too-familiar balk.

"Oh, come on," Jerry pleaded. "This water's *freezing*!"

But Pepper had no intention of coming. Jerry yanked on the chain. Pepper lurched back. "I don't like it one bit more than you do," he grumbled at her, wrapped the lead around the bike's handlebars for better leverage, and heaved again. "Come on!"

Pepper ducked her head stubbornly, and her collar very neatly slipped off her neck and over her head.

"Oh." Jerry gasped. The resultant surge threw him backward. He shifted his footing, and the sharpest of all the stones jabbed into his ankle. He stepped back out of its pointed path, off the edge of the rock bridge, and on another boulder, then fell flat in the water on top of the bicycle with a splashing crash.

Jerry was furious. He wasn't hurt but so angry that he could have spouted fire, despite the freezing cold of the creek. He shouldn't have been so close to the deeper edge! He shouldn't have tried to take both the bike and Pepper across at the same time! Jerry flopped around in the water and snatched at his boots as they floated up to the inky surface, the sleeping bag as it bobbed under his nose, and then the cook pans as they clattered over the rocks. "Blast!" he breathed, as he tossed the lot into the grass. "Pepper!" he shouted. "Where are you?" He pulled the bicycle upright and dragged it to the grass. Water squirted out of the wicker basket as if it were a sieve. Poor old bike; it was surely enduring some rough treatment. He looked across the creek. "Pepper?" he called. Now wherever was she? He started back across the stream to look for her.

Suddenly a blur erupted out of the bush on the opposite bank. It sailed over the stream and right for him. Jerry ducked. Pepper swooped past to land beside the bicycle without dislodging a single blade of grass. But Jerry, standing on the glassy-smooth stones in midstream again, was thrown off balance. He flailed his arms like a fledgling bird, groped for a better footing, slipped again, and toppled back into the deeper creek.

He gasped and crawled to the bank on his hands and knees. Pepper pranced up, playful, and boxed him on the shoulders with sheathed paws. Jerry flung himself down beside her nearly ready to cry with frustration.

Now camping for the night was out of the question. Everything was soaking wet. Everything that is, but Pepper. Whatever were they going to do? The idea of going home was too unbearable to contemplate. He shivered and buckled the collar back on Pepper's neck. Well, he knew the first thing was to dry out, and he had to have a fire to do so. He checked his pack and was pleased to find his waterproof matches were in good shape. The wind rustled the trees and blew over him in cold gusts, making him shiver again. What he needed was some sort of protection, and he hated himself for not having

brought along his small line tent. But he had been in a tearing rush to leave home, and there had been the problem of weight. Jerry sucked in his breath. Pepper's meat! He had forgotten all about it.

Quickly he splashed back into the creek and felt under the dark rippling water for the large packet of food he had been carrying in the wicker basket. Where was it? If only he had a light. But it must have rolled off downstream when he fell, and it was gone. Suddenly his hand touched something long and slick, and he pulled it out of the water. He groaned. It was the wrapping paper that had been around the meat. No need to search any longer. Frozen when he had left home, it must have thawed during the day. To look for chopped meat loose in a rushing stream would be like searching for a grain of wheat loose in a silo of rice. He splashed back ashore. "Well, Pep," he said to the big cat. "You have no choice now. I've nothing for you to eat. Either you learn to catch your own food or get awfully hungry."

But just then Pepper's future problems were of lesser importance than his finding a place in which to spend the remainder of the night. Jerry considered. One of those houses up ahead was owned by a man who eeked out a living by farming. The thought of going straight up to the front door and asking if he could dry out inside the house occurred to him, but Jerry wanted no questions about how he happened to be there in the first place. A ramshackle old barn and some other rickety outbuildings were set back from the farmer's house. Still, Jerry felt he could not trespass into the warmth of the barn's interior either. He remembered a haystack on one corner of the man's cleared land. If he built a fire behind its protective height, invisible to the house, and set up his belongings to dry, he could then burrow into the haystack and sleep out the night.

He collected his gear and they started out. By now the mists had begun to lift, and the rising moon and the glittering stars shone through the scattered clouds, helping his night vision immensely. Soon they reached the top of the mountain they had been climbing, and then began to drop down into its valley. A mile farther on he saw the flicker of a light. If he had not been paying close attention, he might easily have missed it. He pushed the bicycle into a stand of brush to leave until morning, for he certainly didn't want to crash around through the trees pushing it as he looked for the cleared field and the haystack. Then he put his soggy bedroll under one arm and shoved the cook pans into his pack. "Now be still as a mouse," he ordered Pepper, and they began to approach the farm.

Undoubtedly there was a path that led straight to the house, but it was invisible to Jerry. He groped along in the darkness until suddenly the trees parted, and he made out the flatness of a small field. Jumping the poorly graded fire-road ditch, he walked into the clearing. He tugged at a stalk of some sort of farm crop that grew waist high and felt a tufted top. Slowly he walked down one length of the planted plot away from the house. He passed the bulk of the barn, standing darker than even the darkest trees beside it. There were some other shapes, the outbuildings, probably, ghostly in the night. He shivered. Wherever was that haystack? He had circled the field and hadn't found it. Of course, there was always the chance it wasn't even there. He hadn't been up this way since last fall.

He pulled Pepper to a halt. Dare he try the barn? Jerry sighed. No, he couldn't. If Father ever found out, he would skin him. An owl hooted mournfully from the deeper forest. But he was so cold and miserable. For the first time since he had left home he dearly wished he were back and snuggled warmly in his bed. Then Pepper shoved against his leg, and he stood resolute. She must have her chance!

So he couldn't find the haystack, he thought fiercely, and he wouldn't try the barn! But he was going to see if one of those grim little sheds were open and spend the night in one of them. No one would mind, surely. He backtracked, recrossed the edge of the field, and very softly approached the first shack. It was leaning shakily, and when he finally came very close, he saw that it was nothing but a shell. Inside were the remains of the roof and two walls, and he might just as well sleep in a woodpile as there. But the next hutlike building was a bit larger, and he approached it with a little more hope. He touched the walls and felt their roughhewn splintery wood. There was a barnyard smell heavy in the air, and he pulled Pepper around to the opposite side to search for a door.

Suddenly Jerry sucked in his breath. Two huge grunting hogs inside a chicken-wire pen lumbered to their feet and bolted into their grubby house. Well, that place was certainly out! He wasn't going to share a pigsty. He looked across to the one remaining outbuilding that stood very near the barn. What could be in there? Or was it empty? He wondered uneasily just how far it stood from the farmer's house. He couldn't even see the light now, so it was difficult to tell. There was something unlawful about sneaking around someone else's property in the middle of the night, and Jerry felt guilty. But such thoughts vanished as Pepper's chain snapped taut, and he was jerked backward. The pigs were something new to her. They invited more careful investigation.

"Come on!" Jerry whispered. He was anxious to get to that other shed and settle quietly out of sight. Suddenly Pepper leaped onto the roof of the pigsty and nearly pulled Jerry's arm out of his shoulder joint. "Pepper!" Jerry gasped, and pulled at her lead fiercely. She ignored him, put one huge paw on the top sill of the pig's doorway, and took a step down.

Jerry gritted his teeth. If she dropped into that pen he would never get her out. He gripped the chicken-wire fencing, climbed up, and gave a yank on her collar that very nearly pulled off his arm the second time. The tug must have hurt Pepper—she yowled. Jerry bit his lip at the noise, but at least she jumped down on his side of the fence. However, she had sent the two hogs into a frenzy. They were running around inside their covered enclosure and making a terrible racket. He could feel the walls heave and jump with their bumps and shoves. Quickly Jerry reached inside the wire and unlatched the catch that dropped the hatch covering their door. Their squeals instantly became less noticeable, and after a bit they would probably settle down and no doubt be very happy inside for the night.

Jerry pulled Pepper along beside him, and they ran for the remaining shed. It was larger than the pig pen, but there was no fencing. He heaved a sigh. There must not be animals inside. But where was the door? After tugging Pepper all the way around the hut, he came to a halt, puzzled. What was the use of a shed without a door? Pepper nosed something with interest and pulled against her chain. Jerry yanked; Pepper jerked. What was she doing now? She was interested in the bottom edge of the wooden siding, and Jerry bent to see what it was. It was another one of those flaplike doors! Unlike the pig's shed, which had been left open for the pigs to come and go as they pleased, this one was locked. Was there something inside? Jerry pressed one ear to the planking. There was no sound, but it smelled of moss and old mold and the barnyard. The farmer must have locked it shut so the wind wouldn't bang it back and forth. He shivered. The spring breeze was chilling.

Jerry pulled out the wooden peg lock and lifted the small two-foot-square hatchlike door. Bending double, he peered inside. It was dark as ink. By now, however, he was too miserable and too cold to give more than an instant's thought to what might be inside. He dropped on all fours, the only way to get in, and silently shoved himself through the door. For another second he held it open and Pepper slipped through. Then he let it close behind her.

Jerry blinked, opened his eyes wide, and looked hard as he tried to focus on something solid. He turned his head, trying to pick out shapes. Suddenly the hair on his neck prickled. He felt a warm, and living creature right beside him, and it wasn't Pepper. His knees grew weak. The next instant he wished he had dropped over dead.

6 First Lessons

Schraaawk! Chickens! The small enclosure had suddenly become a mass of beating wings and panicked squawks, a mass of bumbling bodies that uttered alarmed clucks and cackles. Everywhere Jerry stepped a white blur erupted before him, and he was thwacked with flailing wings. The dust rose. The pungent smell of wet hair and clothes mixed with that of chickens and grain.

Jerry dropped to his knees, hastily brushed chickens

out of his way, and scrambled along the floor searching for the door. He found it finally, shoved it open, and fell outside into the clean moonlight with a crash. But the door slammed shut on its springs and caught the lead chain while Pepper was still inside the chicken house. Immediately the screaming din within increased to a frenzy.

A light blinked on not far off! His heart thumping, Jerry pushed the door back open, only to be confronted by a squawking chicken with wings spread for faster flight. Quickly he jammed it back into the madhouse and at the same time jerked frantically on Pepper's leash. Now he heard footsteps. Someone was running toward him! Suddenly Pepper squiggled out the hatch. Jerry slammed it closed behind her just as he heard a man shout. Terrified, Jerry snatched Pepper's collar and started to run, but a glance at the mountain lion brought him to a halt in dismay. "Oh, no!" he gasped. Pepper had a chicken in her mouth! He hit her soundly on the head with his fist, and the big cat dropped the terrified hen, which clucked off into the night.

Now they ran like the wind, and Jerry was thankful the moon was fully up and lending light to the darkness around them. He knew the owner of the farm was after them. After a few moments, however, Jerry became aware that the sound he heard at their heels was far faster than that of human feet. He snatched a backward glance. A ghostlike blur was after them. A dog! Not baying, not barking, but racing toward them with lips drawn back to show his vicious teeth. Pepper began to slow, not because she was in the least exhausted from their blind rush through the night, but because she, too, was conscious of the approaching noises and, with her usual curiosity, had decided to stop and see what was there.

"It's a dog!" Jerry hissed at her, as he tried vainly to pull her ahead. But Pepper was not moving. She was determined to investigate. Still, the dog did not bark, and since they were upwind, Pepper could not catch his scent. If she had, Jerry knew she would not be turning back. The animal was momentarily hidden by the thick trees. Pepper looked around inquisitively, and her pursuer flew at her like a bullet.

At the last moment there came a violent crash of underbrush, an upheaval of pine needles, and a sudden scrambling of flying feet reversing their direction. Jerry had been sure the dog was going to attack Pepper. Until the very last moment the animal must have assumed he was giving chase only to a very large dog. When he was nearly nose to nose with Pepper, he recognized what he was about to attack and changed his mind in midlunge. The dog had come very close to Pepper, had swung to one side, banked, slipped in his frenzied haste, and then tumbled head over heels. He scurried back to his feet as fast as he could possibly move and bolted off in the direction from which he had come, squealing in terror. His high, piercing yips echoed fearsomely through the mountains around them.

Pepper's curiosity vanished instantly. The moment the dog gave voice, she realized it was another of those terrible menaces. She turned, in a leap that was quite as terrified as that of the dog, and shot off in the opposite direction. Jerry bobbed along behind her as if he were a feather attached to her chain.

"Buster!" Not far off a man's voice shouted angrily at his dog. "What you doing back here! You go git that varmit!" But Buster was obviously having nothing to do with a full-grown mountain lion. The dog had reached his master, passed him, and raced off to some safer haven. "Come back here!" bellowed the man insistently. There was a curse, an angry mutter, then, unexpectedly, the violent report of a shotgun blast. Pepper put on a further burst of speed, and Jerry flew through the trees like a rocket. He did not really care so long as they put distance between themselves and the farmer. The man had probably shot the gun into the air, a parting gesture now that his dog had fled, in the hope that he might frighten off whatever had been after his chickens. And he had succeeded. Jerry wasn't sure which of them was the more terrified—Pepper or he.

It was blundering good luck that brought them to a halt before a small shed where an engine—the one he had heard hours earlier—chugged away with monotonous regularity. Jerry clutched at the open doorway and sucked in great ragged gasps of breath, for he was badly winded from his run behind the galloping Pepper. They had long since left all sound of the farmer behind them, and as Jerry trembled with fatigue and fright, he was sorry that he had caused the man such concern over his barn-yard. He hadn't meant to upset the hogs or the chickens. All he had wanted was a place to sleep.

Jerry poked his head inside the hut and stared at the motor. It took up nearly all available space, and the heat caused by its endless hours of use enveloped him like a warm blanket. He knew full well this particular engine was not a part of the farmer's belongings. It was the power supply for a small sawmill that was located nearly a mile away. Obviously the mill owner left the engine running day and night.

He pulled Pepper inside, and they stood beside the machine, listening to its gruff rumbles, which soon began to sound very cheerful and cozy. This would be their camp for the night! Jerry unshouldered the pack and methodically spread its contents beside the engine's heated underbody. His belongings were not as wet as he had thought, and a night's drying would take out all their dampness. He had an extra pair of jeans and his slicker, and he put them on, since they were drier than the clothes he was wearing. Over the engine was stretched a wire—presumably on which to hang tools, for on it an oilcan dangled by its handle—and it made a fine clothesline for his wet gear. He unrolled the sleeping bag, unzipped it all around, and spread it above the engine too. His squishy boots and soggy socks he draped over a pipe that protruded from one side of the machine. Everything would be dry by morning. He pulled Pepper close to the engine, and by pushing and pulling at last forced her to lie down so he could curl up beside her and soak up some of her warmth.

The big cat yawned. Apparently she gave her earlier frightening experiences no further thought. But Jerry was unhappy. Nothing was going right. In fact, everything was just awful. He hadn't realized that taking Pepper back to the mountains was going to be such a terribly hard thing to do. Then he remembered that, to add to all his other problems, he hadn't had anything to eat, yet he was too miserable and too tired to root around in the dark looking for the contents of his pack. For a moment he thought of Father and Mother but quickly pushed them out of his mind. He knew they were giving him the opportunity to help Pepper and would expect him to see the attempt through as best he could, no matter what the problems were.

Still, Jerry felt wretched. He pushed his face into Pepper's heavy coat and wiped away the tears that oozed out. Soon Pepper's great body began to vibrate as she growled out her affectionate purr. The oily warm engine chuffed on and on comfortingly. The sounds gave Jerry new heart. Before long he slipped into a deep sleep.

It was first light when he awakened, and he was boiling hot. The combination of Pepper's body heat, the engine, and his slicker made him feel as if he had slept inside an oven. Jerry pushed himself away from the big cat and sat up. He rubbed his eyes and peered around the shed. Something had roused him, something besides suffocating heat. He cocked his head, and as he did Pepper swashed her tongue over his cheek, giving him a wash along with her own morning bath. The engine was what had jarred him into consciousness! It had changed its tune. Now it chuffed more slowly, as if it worked harder. Jerry ran his tongue over his lips nervously and got to his feet. That could mean only one thing. Whoever lived at the sawmill just up the draw had either turned on the water tap or flicked on an electric light. Someone was up, and the time had come for him and Pepper to leave.

Quickly he changed into his brittle-dry clothes and pulled on his creakingly stiff boots. He jammed the pack with the gear that he had strewn about to dry out, then rolled up the sleeping bag. In no more than five minutes he was ready to move. Pepper rubbed her head against his leg and yowled loudly. She was hungry and ready for her breakfast.

"Come on," Jerry whispered. He took a tight grip on her chain, then peered out the door. No one was in sight, but off to the right he saw a faint trickle of silver-white smoke above the pines. Jerry glanced hastily about the shed, made sure he had left nothing behind, and struck out up the fire road. He thought about his bicycle, stuffed inside some scrubby brush back by the farmer's land. It would be safe enough there, and he could come back for it after he returned to Challis. He could not possibly risk going after it. Now, however, he would have to lug all his gear on his back, which would not be much fun on an empty stomach.

But the morning was glorious. The sun was just coming up and shafts of sunlight shown through the trees, setting the dew on the brilliantly green grass to sparkle like diamonds. After a mile or so he stopped beside gurgling Loon Creek and built a small fire. The tang of pine and damp meadows soon mixed with the smell of woodsmoke and frying bacon. He washed up in the creek and then, with a hard heart, tied Pepper to a tree. He ate his meal stolidly, his back to her, and tried very hard not to listen to her heartbreaking wails of hunger. After he had eaten, Jerry cleaned up his camp, put out the fire, and soaked it into a cold and blackened mass with water from the creek.

But didn't he want Pepper to become famished? She had to be terribly hungry before he could teach her to hunt for her own food. Jerry bit his lip as he shouldered his pack. Perhaps Father was right. How could he ever watch Pepper suffer through near starvation? He un-snapped her chain. There was no need to keep her on a lead any longer. Civilization had ended at the sawmill. Ahead of them lay only the vast wilderness.

They started off again, and as Jerry trudged along he went over what little information he had in his mind on how to teach mountain lions to hunt. The only thing he was sure of was that they had to be taught by their mother when they were very young. But how a mother mountain lion did so, Jerry had no idea. He suspected she found her kits an easy prey, then let them fumble about on their own and hopefully bring it down. When he was sitting beside Pepper's house at home, it had seemed easy to him. Now that he must actually begin, however, he had no idea of how to start. And he had Pepper's age to deal with, too. She wasn't a kitten. She also had been brought up never to hurt anything.

Jerry chewed at his lip as he thought about the old hen at the chicken coop last night and how Pepper had held it in her mouth unhurt. How was he ever going to unteach everything she had learned over the past two years? Suddenly he realized that Pepper must kill! He had been stupid ever to have thought she could do anything else and survive, yet he had put the bloody part of the business out of his mind because he hadn't wanted to think about it.

Jerry stopped and picked up a likely-looking hiking stick, tested it this way and that for heft, and then scanned the way before him. Here he had to leave Loon Creek and take to the higher country. Easy traveling along the stream had come to an abrupt end, for the sides of the creek now stood out rocky, precipitous, and impassible. They would become even more treacherous as the creek wound its way through the rocky land until it finally poured from a cataract into the Middle Fork of the Salmon River some five miles away. Jerry knew climbers had made their way along Loon Creek from this point on, but he had always gone by way of the trail past hulking Sleeping Deer Mountain.

His eyes picked out Pepper, who had begun to roam now she was off her lead. She loved the open country. Finding her way along the rocks and boulders, she leaped from precipice to precipice beside the raging creek with surefooted nonchalance. From a distance no one would ever guess that she wasn't wild: heavily built, rippling with powerful muscles, yowling. Though Jerry could not hear her voice over the bubble of the creek, he saw the glint of her teeth. She certainly looked ferocious standing up there.

Jerry whacked the hiking stick at a clump of grass and knocked it flat. If he hadn't known Pepper was just a big baby, he would be more than alarmed at the sight of her roaming so close to his path. For the barest second a thought flashed through Jerry's mind. *Was* that Pepper up there? But as he stared hard at the ledge on which the mountain lion stood, the animal vanished as if at the wave of a magician's wand. Jerry shook his head sharply and struck out up the path. Now *that* was the silliest thought ever! Of course, the mountain lion had been Pepper. She was just up to her usual trick of appearing in the most unlikely places. Out here in the cougar country she had momentarily taken on the appearance of one of her wilder sisters.

Soon enough she reappeared, bobbing out of the underbrush and wailing at him with more persistence than ever. "I know. You're starving," Jerry said, as he patted her head. "I didn't plan for you to go totally without food. If I hadn't lost your meat in the creek, I'd at least give you a taste." Jerry considered feeding her a bit from his own supplies, but a butterfly suddenly flicked out of the bunchgrass beside the path, and Pepper was after it in a second. Jerry followed close behind and whacked at it with his hiking stick, trying to help her make a catch. Pepper soon lost interest, however, and sat down and began to howl unhappily. Still, Jerry kept right on and eventually was able to bring the butterfly down.

"Pepper," he called to her, but by that time she was scratching at a tree's sturdy trunk, sharpening her claws. Jerry carried the butterfly over to her. She stopped scratching and lifted her muzzle to the insect. "Eat it," Jerry said insistently and tossed the dead thing at her feet. Once more Pepper nosed the butterfly, then raised her eyes to Jerry and, with an impatient flick to the tip of her tail, wailed piercingly. Jerry unshouldered the pack, took out his camp plate, and placed it on the ground before her. Instantly Pepper came to attention. A dish meant food, and she rubbed against Jerry's legs nearly tumbling him over, as she purred throatily. He placed the butterfly in the middle of the plate. "Well, there's your breakfast," he told her grimly. Pepper stared at the wingy morsel, sniffed it, cast a bored glance at the surrounding brush, wheeled back to the plate to sniff again, and at last ate. Jerry stuffed the dish back into the pack and started out up the trail.

Pepper roared unhappily. "Well, if you're so hungry, then go find another," he told her. "Butterflies are better to eat than nothing." He kicked at a bush, hoping to see another flutter out of the leaves. Then Jerry eyed the earth at his feet, and pointed. "Pepper, look! Here are some ants." They were big red ants, and they poured in and out of their gravelly hill with bustling industry.

Pepper came up, shoved her nose to the ground, twitched her whiskers at the creeping multitude, then exhaled violently, blowing dust and insects into the air and Jerry's face. "Catch them!" he said angrily. "You can eat ants, you know!" He forced one between her dark lips, but Pepper shook her head, flicked out her tongue, and spat it out. "Eat it!" Jerry ordered and once more stuffed an insect between her immense teeth. "For crying out loud, must you have them on a plate, too?" He yanked the dish back out of his pack and methodically began to collect squashed ants.

The few minutes were not very enjoyable, nor were the insects at all eager to be made into a meal. "Yeeouch!" Jerry rubbed his fingers on his trouser leg. The ants bit fiercely. "Here, Pepper," he called, once he had massed a sufficient number to be noticeable on the tin plate. Pepper sniffed, ignored the menu for a long moment, finally sniffed again, then reluctantly licked them up. But the new taste made her leap to her feet, toss her head furiously, lash out with her tongue, show her teeth, growl, shake her head again, then run up the path at a full gallop. Jerry sighed. Obviously red ants were not to be her favorite food.

The sun climbed above the trees and shone down warmly on the clearly marked path. It was a precipitous trail, and Jerry soon became damp with perspiration despite the cold of the high altitude. Gradually the path changed from brown, packed earth to a cracked and weathered gray stone, and the trees, which had grown steadily more sparse, clumped in dwarfed and isolated windswept groups until finally there were none at all. Then they came across the first patches of late melting snow where rivulets of dark water trickled from beneath the puckered ice edges. Still the path climbed, the snowy plots grew more numerous, and temperatures fell below freezing.

Jerry stopped, shaded his eyes with his cupped hand, and stared into the heights of Sleeping Deer Mountain that jutted up lonely and desolate at his feet. Small dark cloud patches formed around the deeper clefts of the towering precipices, and now and then a puff of powder snow swirled into the air where it was whisked away into nothing. In the silent stillness Jerry heard the faint moan of wind, for up there it blew endlessly. He shivered and pushed on. The mountain seemed to loom threatening and unfriendly when he was alone, and it hovered over him in moody sullenness.

A few minutes later Jerry faced a problem he had not expected. Their trail ahead was blocked with snow, an immense quantity that had toppled during the winter from one of the higher pinnacles in a huge avalanche. It had surged over the path, down and down, until it met the stand of trees at timberline. Their aged strength had been unable to withstand such a tremendous force, and they had cracked before it like matchsticks. Jerry looked in dismay at the trail ahead. It was gone. It was lost beneath tons of ice and snow and would doubtless remain so for months to come. Perhaps it would never reappear, and the first winter snows would only add to its covering blanket.

Pepper loped up and nosed the hulk of ice and rock that blocked their way. She scratched at it interestedly, seemed to decide it was only another overlarge rocky face, and nimbly leaped to the top. As far as Jerry could see, the only way he could continue his trek into the wilderness was to scale the slippery mass, cross the icy crest, then find the path again on the other side of the avalanche. He wished he possessed Pepper's agility and could leap to the top in a half-dozen bounds. Chiseling out a stair-stepping ladder in the ice with his knife was slow and tedious work.

Much later he finally pulled himself over the highest ledge of the avalanche and stood upright. There he stopped and stared, openmouthed and aghast, at the scarred world around him. The landslide had made a terrible mess of the mountainside. It was a grim, grimy white, blotched with gravelly mud and rocks. Dribbles of water ran around ridges and boulders, while below him broken pines protruded from the ice at all angles as if they'd been set helter-skelter by an invisible giant. Walking across the top layer was tricky, for not only was the surface slippery, some of the deeper cracks and crevasses looked dark and treacherous.

When he came up to Pepper, he found she wasn't resting while she waited for him as he had thought. Instead, she was deeply absorbed in watching a burrow that had been bored into the ice. She squatted on all fours and moved her tail this way and that, occasionally giving its very tip a flick. The hole into which she stared so intently obviously belonged to some sort of rodent. Small footprints left in the snow showed its comings and goings. Jerry's heart began to beat faster. If Pepper could catch the animal as it came out, she would have the chance to taste fresh meat. The experience could be the beginning of her return to the wilderness. He dropped his pack, gripped his hiking stick like a club, and took up a watch beside the cat. She might need his help.

Jerry had no idea how long they waited. But it was long enough for him to get thoroughly cold and the knees of his pants wet and soggy. During their watch he brooded thoughtfully over the tiny animal that must be quaking in terror beneath the ice. The little thing hadn't hurt anyone, least of all Pepper or himself. If the owner of the burrow was one of those hoary marmots, he would be fat and furry as a cuddly brown Teddy bear. Or perhaps it was one of the gray-brown, rabbitlike conys with tiny round ears and no tails that scurried here and there, doing nothing more vicious than collecting bits and pieces of dried grass. Jerry felt his hold on the hiking stick waver. He knew that being hunted by the likes of Pepper was a natural part of such an animal's life, and this moment was probably not the first a killer had waited outside his doorstep. Jerry rested his forehead on the ice and closed his eyes. Nature wasn't very kind, really. Behind her beauty always lurked a cold ruthlessness.

Unexpectedly a clatter of stones jarred Jerry upright. He gasped. Over the top edge of the avalanche appeared a full-grown bighorn sheep. "Wow!" he whispered, staring at the heavily built animal with its massive backward-curving horns. Suddenly another appeared and another, and then a lamb babbled lustily. What a sight! Jerry had never seen bighorns so near, and he gawked at them in sheer pleasure.

But he had forgotten Pepper. The cat leaped up at his feet, the burrow in the ice forgotten on the instant, and she bounded toward the new visitors. But the startled flock had seen her, and as Jerry got to his feet they turned tail and disappeared back over the side of the avalanche they had so lately come up. Jerry snatched up his pack and ran, slipping and sliding after Pepper, to catch a last glimpse of them. Then he slowed. He had been mistaken about all the sheep having fled. There was one that remained. It was the big leader, the one with the immense horns and the weatherbeaten coat, splotchy with his spring shedding. He had stayed behind as the flock's protector, and he turned to meet Pepper's advance without a waver.

Jerry stood still. A performance began to unfold before him that at first had the appearance of a comic dance. The sheep, instantly alert, appeared to perch motionless on hoof tips, prepared to dart in any direction. Pepper crossed the distance between them like a silken shadow. She stopped, stretched out her long neck to sniff in inquiry, then stood poised as though she were ready to dive from a springboard. A second later the bighorn shifted infinitesimally backward, and Pepper lifted one paw, flicked her tail once, then froze into place. A moment passed until the sheep, as if worked by a mechanical spring, dipped his head the barest fraction to display to Pepper a thick front of horned might. Pepper opened her mouth, showed her teeth unpleasantly, and put the lifted paw back to the ground, then stood rock still. Another breathless moment elasped. At last the bighorn shifted another few inches backward, Pepper lifted the other

front paw, flicked her tail imperceptibly, twitched her face, and again stood motionless.

A deathlike stillness prevailed during this fancy footwork. Despite her appearance of slow motion, Pepper had somehow managed to come very close to the brawny sheep. The sheep seemed to be balanced on the very edge of the avalanche, half on ice, half in space. And now an electricity charged the air. Jerry was uneasy. The bighorn's resolution to protect the flock and fight to the death, if need be, apparently had transformed Pepper's first reaction of frisky curiosity. Jerry wanted to break the spell that held the two animals. The sight of the Pepper he had known disappearing before him into a killer was almost more than he could bear. He hadn't a chance to consider more closely that this situation was exactly the one he had hoped to bring about when he left home. Nor had he time to intervene.

There was a sudden squeak of ice underfoot, and both animals appeared to leap straight up. Which of the two moved first was impossible for Jerry to tell. But the bighorn came to earth in a great lunge forward, caught Pepper with his great, cruel horns, threw her into the air, and out over the edge of the avalanche. The sheep turned instantly to face him, and for a terrified moment Jerry was sure the animal was about to charge. But no—the mountain lion was the dreaded enemy and had been dealt with safely. He turned from Jerry, trotted up the avalanche, and disappeared from sight.

Jerry threw himself on his stomach and inched to the edge of the clifflike ice over which Pepper had disappeared. If she hadn't been gored to death, the fall to the rocks of the mountainside below would have crushed her.

"Oh, Pepper!" he choked and looked down the nearly sheer face of ice.

7 The Protector

Jerry should have realized a cat always lands on its feet.
Pepper was sitting below him on a soft patch of snow,
nonchalantly giving herself a good wash. Her tongue
swiped at her chest as she busily smoothed out her ruffled
coat, and when Jerry let out a breath of relief, Pepper
looked up at him and yowled. Her flight through space
had not bothered her nearly as much as the growlings of
her empty stomach.

It took all morning for Jerry to find a way down from the heights of the avalanche. Even then most of his descent was accomplished by slipping and sliding on the seat of his pants. By the time he finally was able to start out on the path again it was almost noon. Clouds, thicker than those hovering over the mountain, began to form, dark and foreboding. He started to hurry, not wanting to be caught above timberline in a spring thunderstorm. There was nearly a mile left to go before the trail began to drop to the river, and he couldn't hurry over it. The climb was steep, and the altitude made him breathless. The slick, mica-flecked trail was sprinkled with bits of shale that felt as if marbles had been sprinkled underfoot. He thought he knew what an astronaut felt like stalking along the barren, rock-strewn moon. This high mountainside resembled that lifeless place—nothing grew, nothing moved. The only sound was that of the wind and the clatter of his cook pans as now and then he shifted his pack.

But at last he reached the summit, and as he stood for a moment to wipe the perspiration from his forehead he looked across the expanse before him. Right off he could tell he was not going to stay dry. Rain already slanted over the craggy cliffs across the gorge ahead of him. Even as he watched, lightning flashed unpleasantly over the trees.

The path went downhill now, and Jerry hesitated only long enough to try and chain Pepper. She was no fonder of thunderstorms than he was. At home she was always allowed inside the house whenever one passed over and hid beneath his bed or squeezed behind the sofa. Jerry did not want her to bolt suddenly in terror on this trip. To try to find a frightened mountain lion in this wilderness would be an impossibility. Yet if she did run away terrified, he could not leave her. So far he had proven Pepper would only starve to death. But the big cat would not let herself be leashed. Each time Jerry approached she ducked her head and ran out of reach, and there was no time to waste playing catch-me-if-you-can games. It was important to get down off the sheer face of the mountain and into the scrub where the rough country was littered with deep clefts and canyons. There innumerable cliffy niches offered shelter from the rapidly approaching storm.

Pepper shot off ahead, and Jerry soon lost sight of her as he half trotted, half ran down the steep incline. Occasionally through the trees he caught sight of the faint sparkle of silver that was the Middle Fork of the Salmon River as it snaked its way through the rocky canyon. He reached the first sprinkling of pines and firs that grew, dwarfed and twisted, at timberline. Within moments the trail became packed earth. Beside it grass had found sufficient soil in which to root, and as it emerged from

the melting snow, showed brilliantly green, while tiny
yellow flowers dotted it like flecks of gold. Now the
dusty dampness of fresh rain came sweeping in to him on
the wind. Jerry watched it advance toward him in sheets of
smoky gray.

Then Pepper reappeared. She ran toward him, and for
a moment Jerry gaped at her, startled. The cat's lips were
drawn back, her whiskers bristled. Whatever had she seen
that raised her hackles so? Or was it only that a storm was
coming and she had no place to hide? Jerry made another
last frantic snatch for her collar, missed, and then stood
for a second glaring at her as she circled him, snarling
slightly, just out of reach. Lightning flashed. Thunder
crashed.

"Come here!" Jerry ordered sharply. But the cat only
flattened her ears, snarled again, and dashed off down the
path. "Oh, blast you anyway!" Jerry shouted and started
after her at a run, slipped once and nearly pitched into a
rocky ditch before he caught himself and careened on.
Soon she reappeared again, ears still flattened tightly
against her head. Jerry was sure she dearly wanted to
come to him but refused, because she knew if she did he
would leash her. Another flash of lightning. Pepper
leaped as if shot, left the path, and bolted into a rocky
gully. She bounded from crag to crag, boulder to boulder.

Jerry slid to a stop. He couldn't go on and leave her. And perhaps Pepper was showing better sense than he was himself. She was threading her way along the clifflike hillside where here and there huge rocks and great slabs of stone had toppled and fallen, forming dark-looking protective shelters. Jerry glanced at the oncoming torrent, then back to Pepper. She was stopped now, perched on a rock, and stared back at him as if to say, "Hurry up! It's going to pour!" Even as he watched she looked up, and following her glance Jerry saw an outcropping of rock that had formed a sort of overhanging protective roof. He squinted at the big cat. She was still all abristle. The hair along her back was up, her ears still flattened, and her teeth showed. He could tell she was spitting and hissing sharply, a sure sign that she was on edge. She certainly missed the front-room davenport under which she could hide. But that half shelter she had found seemed as if it might offer some refuge from the rain.

Jerry left the path and picked his way through the rocks and brush. The boulders were huge, and it was difficult to keep Pepper in sight. She was well camouflaged. Her coat was nearly the same color as the buff-colored rocks, and the black lichen that partly covered the uneven ledges matched the moustache marks on her face. Raindrops began to patter all around and splotched the stone with sooty spots. As they sprinkled at his feet, he could see Pepper had left her footprints behind in the dust.

"I do hope you've picked a good spot," Jerry panted, when he finally reached the rock on which the cat stood. "It's going to rain buckets!" He shrugged on his slicker as he climbed the face of the ledge. Pepper peered down at him, and as he pulled off his pack and tossed it up beside her she spit, hissed, and growled. "It's only a thunderstorm," Jerry said soothingly, wedging himself between two big rocks in order to gain more leverage as he inched straight up. "This didn't look so steep from over there," he said with a gasp.

Suddenly the rain began to crash through the trees like an express train. The pines whirled and bent to the blast. The scrub bobbed and dipped like maddened dancers. Jerry snatched Pepper's tail as it hung down the rock directly in front of him and, using it as a handhold, dragged himself the last few feet to the entrance of the sheltered lodge. Pepper dropped instantly and crouched in front of him to lie on his feet as the rain poured down on her unmercifully.

"Come on," Jerry shouted, as he stumbled over her. Lightning slashed into the trees beside the trail he had just left. Pepper leaped up as the thunder cracked with a deafening crash. Like two frightened deer they flung themselves back into the protection of the rock.

Jerry pressed himself against the stone and tried to stop the trembling in his knees. He surely did hate lightning! Suppose it started a fire. That would be all he needed, to have a forest fire burst up in front of him. He reached down to touch Pepper, cheered that at least he had her for company.

But the cat wasn't there! Jerry pushed himself away from the rock and looked down at his feet. "Pepper?" He stepped forward and looked out the shelter's entrance. Surely she hadn't gone back out in that monsoon! He turned. There was another huge rock beside him, and space between it and the cliff face. She must have wedged herself in there. Jerry dropped to his knees, muddying his pants in the process, and looked in the crack.

"Pepper?" She wasn't there either. He crept to the other side of the boulder. She must have squeezed through the smaller opening on that side and gone farther back into the cliff. "Pepper?" Jerry inched past the rock and gasped. A cave! Well, it was a sort of half cave made by a deep cleft in the mountainside and covered over by rocks that most probably had tumbled down thousands of years ago. Daylight seeped in here and there, for the huge boulders wedged against the clifflike face weren't solidly filled in. Water from the rain pattered and trickled among the stones.

But wherever was Pepper? There wasn't much space

overall, but the cavelike room was very, very high, with stair-stepping rocks and boulders and hidden ledges. "Pep? Here, Pep." He squinted in the dim light, looked high, and tried to focus on definite shapes. A lightning flash outside illuminated the room for the briefest second and after an instant's glimpse of dun-colored, dusty rock he was blinder than ever. The cat was obviously cowering behind one of those boulders.

Jerry stood up and took a cautious step forward. "Pepper, wherever are you?" In response came a slight, light movement. "Don't fret, girl," he said cheerily. "The storm's already going past." In reply came a faint, low sound. Jerry stopped. He ran his tongue over his lips, then cocked his head, listening hard. "Pep?" A muffled, low-pitched growl and then a rumbling cough whispered back at him. Jerry gasped and took a step backward, coming up hard against wet rock. The hair on his neck prickled and stood out. That wasn't Pepper. Never in her life had she made such a sound.

Jerry's mind urged him to run from the cave, yet his body refused to move. He stared horrified into the gloom while his heart thumped wildly. He heard the splash of water as it dribbled from rock to rock, crevice to crevice, the mournful whisper of the wind in the cracks and clefts high overhead, the soft tick-tick of his watch on the wrist he had flung to his face. He smelled freshly dampened

dust, pine whipped by the wind, rubbery rain jacket, decay, and wetted fur. Pepper! She must be close. Soaking from the rain, she would smell like a wet dog.

Jerry turned, coming to life as quickly as he had frozen seconds before. He moved toward the cave entrance cautiously, uncertain what animal besides Pepper was there. Slowly his eyes became used to the darkness, and shapes began to emerge: bluff boulders, craggy rocks. And then, between him and safety, he saw a soft blur of movement. He halted in midstep.

Like a pair of ghosts, two mountain lions materialized, etched against the darkness. Their eyes glowed wickedly amber as they faced each other with deadly intent. One of them was Pepper—which one Jerry could not tell. The light was too poor to see her collar, his only sure means of identification. One of them stood on a tall slab of rock and looked down; the other was half crouched ready to spring upward. Their heads were small, rounded globes, with ears flattened tightly against their skulls. From each came a low-pitched sound, part growl, part hiss, part snarl.

Jerry was trapped. To reach the safety of the open mountainside he needed to pass between the two animals. And he was not so foolhardy as to try such a maneuver. Never in his life had he been so frightened. Father! He needed Father! But help was far away.

A cricket suddenly shrilled into song. Jerry swallowed. The cat on the rocky pedestal had raised one front leg and swung it up as if to ward off a blow. Claws were bared viciously, although Pepper seldom unsheathed hers. Could that cat possibly be she? Or was Pepper the other animal, who, with the faintest tremble of its body, suddenly shot upward with all the speed of a loosed arrow?

Jerry screamed; he stepped back, stumbled, and fell to his knees just as the two animals met in midair. They dropped heavily to the earth, and Jerry's ears were filled with roaring, throaty snarls and growls. Dust flew into his face. He shrank further into the shadows as the two animals suddenly sprang apart, then as quickly closed in again. They rolled toward him, twisting, turning, and then rolled away again. With all the weight of a swung ax, a heavy tail slashed across Jerry's arm. Now they were apart. Again they charged each other and balled into a ferocious curled shape as one tried to claw the underbelly of the second. They broke apart, fenced with lightning-fast forepaws, and met again. Their bawl of fury was deafening.

And then one was gone—vanished like a shadowy phantom. Jerry flung his hands to his face. He still couldn't get out! The remaining cat blocked his way. Suddenly the animal whirled on him, ready to attack. Jerry knew the end had come. He couldn't scream. He couldn't even move. The cat approached him low to the ground, like some evil snake. The beast's head lifted and came for his face.

It was wet. The swipe of that affectionate tongue and the purr that growled deep inside Pepper's chest was pleasure. She nuzzled against Jerry's neck and licked him again and again. She pushed against his legs, her tail held high, and wound her arched back around him in her typical, loving, pussycat way. She shoved her head into his hands expectantly, waiting for Jerry to find her favorite scratching place.

"Pep!" Jerry gasped. "I thought—I thought you were the other one!" Pepper pushed more insistently than ever against his hand. "Oh, we have to get out of here!" He heaved the cat aside and lurched for the entrance. With his right hand he dragged his pack along; with the left he pulled Pepper. That the other mountain lion might still be hovering just outside never crossed his mind. He staggered into the open, pitched over the rocky face he had taken so long to ascend earlier, and slid down the cliff headfirst. When he came to a rough-and-tumble halt he leaped to his feet, released Pepper, and bolted for the trail. Once there he ran full tilt toward the river.

Jerry stopped at last, not wanting to, but forced by sheer fatigue. His breath came in great noisy gulps, and he clutched his side, which ached as if it had been pierced by a dagger. He hesitated only a moment and was up again, staggering on drunkenly. Finally exhaustion brought him to a halt once more, and with it came the realization that the other beast could have overtaken him easily if it had wanted to. Jerry flung himself to the ground and looked back. There were only trees with thick skirts of impenetrable brush. No sign of living thing was evident, yet when his panting breath became less noisy, he tensed. What was that sound, that constant, muffled humming? It was eerie.

Suddenly Pepper, who had disappeared down the path as she passed him on his panicked flight, came bobbing up again. Jerry snatched her collar. But Pepper was unhappy. She yanked away from him, snarled, showed her teeth, then let out one of her terrifying, ear-piercing screams. It reverberated through the trees. Jerry clenched his teeth and closed his eyes tightly. He was positive there was nothing on earth more blood-curdling or hair-raising than Pepper's scream.

"Don't do that!" he groaned. She sat down suddenly and began to cry pitifully. Her empty stomach was causing her constant misery.

In a few moments Jerry got to his feet and went on. He wished he was not enclosed by the heavy brush and the aged, tall pines that were so thick he could not even see the sky. The path turned abruptly, and the way ahead opened. Pepper nearly knocked him down as she surged past, but Jerry hardly noticed. He stopped in the clearing, and though he had been in the very same spot at other times, he always was stunned by the spectacle that stretched before him.

He was standing on a high bank some eighty feet above the Middle Fork of the Salmon River, and he looked out over the tops of pines that grew along the riverbank. The river wormed into the sunset between sheer rocky banks, and far, far beyond, as it made a turn, the snowcapped hazy mountains that formed its left bank jutted up, seeming to block its way. It was beautiful. Directly below him the water was a murky greenish brown and riddled with wind ripples and swirls of eddies. Jerry made a face. That frightening sound he had heard was only the voice of the river. He ought to have known; he had heard it often enough. He hated to admit it, but he longed to catch other sounds, too—a voice raised in a cheery hallo, a rattle of a hiking boot on stone. But there was nothing. Only the sigh of the river as it moved away from him.

Pepper brought him back to earth as she touched his hand and cried for her meal. He stroked her head and scratched her chin, but she wasn't in the mood for his affection. She wanted food. She pulled away from him with a snarl and ran down the path that dropped off steeply at his feet. It was a brown line etched through round blackish rocks that had long ago fallen from above. In a moment she reappeared, far ahead, only a small figure that loped away from him. The sight of her leaving him filled Jerry with loneliness, and he dashed down the trail to catch up.

8 Hunter

Jerry spent another disagreeable night, and all because of
Pepper. She was as restless as if she had been imprisoned
in a cage. She paced—back and forth, back and forth—
beside his sleeping bag, and time after time Jerry was
jarred awake by the sound of a sharply snapping twig. He
would sit up with his heart thumping unpleasantly and
find it was only the big cat walking, walking, casting dis-
quieting shadows onto the sand in the dying firelight.

After a few moments to calm his nerves, he would toss another log on the fire, the sparks spattering into the darkness, and call to her. But when she came, she snarled and spit and perhaps cried. She never lay down at his feet as she usually did at night, nor did she allow him to touch her. Each time she turned away and paced her dozen steps, turned and paced the same ones back—whirl and repeat, whirl and repeat. Pepper might as well have been chained.

Jerry lay unsleeping for a long while and thought of her. Now he knew why she had been all abristle and strange up there on the hill. She had known there was another mountain lion up there somewhere. Pepper was always snappish and prickly when she was around ordinary house cats, which should have tipped him off. And he should have known that once the battle in the cave was finished, he had nothing to fear from the other cougar. Pepper had been victorious. The other had run away in defeat and would not return to fight again for a long time.

Jerry breathed in the sweet scent of smoke and pine, closed his eyes, and tried to sleep. He hadn't thought Pepper could ever fight a battle, let alone win it. Any animal born wild and raised as Pepper had been was balanced delicately between the two worlds. Jerry knew she loved him, yet now, away from civilization, she was teetering toward wildness. Hungry nearly past endurance, she was trying in her way to pull free of the invisible bonds that held her to him. Up there on the high mountainside, her love for him and an instinct to protect him had forced her to fight. For a few brief minutes her wild nature had taken over. Jerry's heart ached. He knew he was losing her.

Finally he slept, but at first light awoke shivering. He pulled on his socks and boots and tugged his jacket collar higher. The day might be blazing hot, yet the morning was certainly freezing cold. There was no sign of Pepper, and he wondered how long she had been away from camp. He shrugged the pack over his shoulders and picked up his hiking stick. And then Pepper was there. She materialized soundlessly out of the underbrush just beyond the river's edging of sand. Coming to him she wailed hungrily. Jerry listened to her callously. The rattle of the camp pans had been as clear a call to her as if he had spoken her name.

"You know, Pepper, today's the day you learn how to catch something to eat." For an answer she thrust her face into his hand and flung it upward. He felt the wetness of her lips and her stickery whiskers. Finally he weakened. "I'll make a compromise," he said, as he struck out up the beach. "I'll not eat breakfast, since you can't. And that's a promise," he said firmly.

As they left the miles behind them, the country grew rougher. It was treacherous, too, with loose stones and jagged rocks. They were enclosed by the mountains that jutted up on both sides of the riverbanks, so followed the shoreline as much as possible, leaving it only when the water, swollen from the spring thaws, forced them to higher ground.

On one of these upper ledges Jerry saw a deer far in the distance. Quickly he gripped Pepper by the collar and tried to force her eyes in its direction. But she didn't see it among the distant rocks nor when the deer waded into the water, deeper, deeper, until it was forced to swim. The current caught the big animal and sucked it downstream swiftly, but within moments it touched the bottom on the other side. It lurched out to the bank, then disappeared into the rocks and trees.

Another time they saw an eagle. Jerry, his eyes shaded with his hand, thought its eyrie was located on one of the craggy cliffs. There were small clefts up there, and probably in one of them the beautiful bird had built its nest. Pepper gazed up at it lazily as it soared overhead, and Jerry wondered if she remembered that day, long ago, when she had nearly been carried off by the hawk.

About the time the sun was ready to sink behind the cliffs on the western shore, Jerry turned up a well-beaten animal track and within a few minutes left the river's roar behind. For the first time in a long while, Jerry heard the trill of a bird and the soft breath of wind as it whispered in the pines. After a half hour they climbed a small ridge and came upon the meadow where he planned to camp for the night. Usually when Jerry saw it the grass was yellowed and dry, but now it was a soft, delicate green. The brush was in bloom and colored a dusky, silvery gray, and the blue mountain lupine checkered the green like a patchwork quilt. It was so pretty that Jerry swung his pack off his shoulder and, carrying it in one hand, ran down into the grass. Pepper, invigorated by the cool freshness of the late afternoon, bounced just ahead in her familiar hobbyhorse manner.

Suddenly there was a flurry of wings nearly under their feet. Jerry gasped as a half-dozen sage grouse flew straight up. Pepper reared back on her hind legs, as startled as the hens, and began to box at the thrashing brown forms as they flashed past. Jerry swung the pack, frightened one of the birds, and it cascaded into Pepper's reaching paws. There was a tangle of fur, a squawk, and grass and feathers and little gray flowers flew all around. In an instant the kill was over. Jerry stared down at a decapitated bird that lay at Pepper's feet and marveled at the way she instantly picked it up and carried it off a little distance, dragging it between her two front legs like any wild lion.

At that moment the Pepper Jerry had always known vanished before his eyes. She was still there, ripping the bird apart, flicking feathers from the flesh, eating it with relish, but she no longer was his pet, a part of him, as she had been. Jerry turned away, dragged his pack through the grass, and when he stood before the place where he planned to spend the night, the sight of a recent campfire scarcely penetrated his consciousness. Later, when the big cat came to him, Jerry saw that she was anxious to be off.

It was long after dark when Pepper finally appeared again, and Jerry's breath caught, for she dropped another sage hen at her feet. She stood just outside the ring of firelight and looked in at him, her amber eyes flashing. The bond between them was broken now. She knew it and lay down in the grass to eat away from him. Jerry swallowed and poked at the coals with his hiking stick, firing the end, then dousing it in the damp earth, then repeating the process again and again. She could feed herself, and she could fight sufficiently well for protection. Her need of him was gone. He tried not to think of winter's approach. It was still a long way off, with time for her to learn her own lessons of survival.

Now the next step, painful as it was for Jerry to think about, was clearly indicated. The time had come to leave her. Once she had killed she mustn't return to civilization. She was wild, like her mountain sisters. What he had done frightened Jerry slightly, and yet it pleased him, too.

Morning came with mists. Jerry sat up and stared at the

cold campfire, and after a moment he decided against lighting it and fixing a hot breakfast. Pepper wasn't about, and it might be a good time for him to get under way and leave her behind. Though this was not the exact place he had planned for her, it was just as good. There was the river for water, all those sage grouse for food, and he had seen a deer not too far away. He knew the hills held thousands of niches in which she could find a warm place to live. Putting his face in his hands, he wished that he were home. Parting was not easy. Then he thought of Judge Bailey and the sheriff, and then of Uncle Frank's cage and Old Muddy. Worse than that, he remembered that awful dog pound on Central Avenue where they put the sick animals to sleep.

Jerry packed his gear silently, slipped on his boots, and tiptoed through the grass. After a while he picked up the trail on the ridge. Every now and then his boots clattered on stone and he stopped, listening, wondering if Pepper had heard. He had gone well over an hour before the sun began to burn off the fog, and as he tried dismally to forget Pepper he thought about going home. His heart beat faster at all he had to recount to Father and Mother. But he still had a long way to go. He estimated it was nearly ten miles before he would reach the ranger station on Shuman's Peak. From there he would pick up the fire road, which eventually would lead him to the main road and back to Challis an entirely different way.

Suddenly Jerry sucked in his breath, thoughts of home instantly forgotten. There on the ridge behind him was Pepper. He hadn't left her behind after all. Jerry chewed at his lip. She was wandering all over the mountainside investigating, glancing up every so often to keep him within sight. He made a face. His sneaky start had been useless.

By noontime she was still about. Jerry longed for her to come close, yet he forced himself to keep her at a distance and not call her name. She had managed to get ahead of him over the hours and kept popping up in unexpected places, sometimes within yards of him, sometimes almost out of sight in the distance. Jerry began to worry whether he could manage to leave her at all. She was roaming far, and though she no longer needed him, she still seemed to feel a want to keep him in reserve. He had to break her of that habit lest he lead her back to civilization.

Eventually Jerry came to the edge of an exceptionally deep canyon. Before descending into it, he found a patch of grass that looked warm and inviting and stopped for lunch. He scrounged through his pack for something edible. There wasn't a great deal left. There were those hard crackers that ought to have been eaten only with something like soup. But he didn't feel like starting a fire, for if he did, Pepper might decide to come closer. Then he would have to force her away, and he didn't want to do so. Well, what else did he have? Dry milk. He got out the tin cup and poured a bit of the powder into it. Next he unscrewed the lid of the canteen and, as he did, glanced up and looked below him.

Not far away Pepper had stopped on top of a flat boulder nearly twice her size. She was poised in her old perched position, with her four paws nearly touching, and she was looking up at him. Jerry wished she hadn't caught him eating. He wouldn't want her to think he might feed her again. His heart ached for her. He began to stir the milk to mix it with the water. What a terrible lunch—hardtack and half-diluted milk! He watched Pepper turn around as if she was ready to come up and join him. Quickly he gulped the biscuit, anxious to finish, and lifted the cup to drink, when a rifle cracked in the still mountain air. He stared transfixed with horror as Pepper immediately collapsed on the rock.

Jerry dropped the cup, and milk spilled down his jacket. His thoughts shot back to last night's used campfire. Subconsciously he had realized that other people were in the mountains nearby. Even as he started to run down the hill toward Pepper, he saw the two hunters. But Pepper was struggling to get to her feet. Jerry thrashed through the brush. He swept pine branches out of his way. One of the men had a gun raised, and it was aimed at Pepper as she tried to stand.

"No!" Jerry screamed. "Stop!" He fell, slid down in the rocks, then flew to his feet, and plunged on. "Don't shoot!" he shrieked. "Stop!" Pepper had toppled over again and, to his horror, now lay motionless. Below him the two men turned and looked at him, with disbelief on their faces. "Don't shoot!" Jerry screamed at them again. He leaped over a stand of brush and down onto the big boulder beside the prostrate cat. Pepper's eyes were only partially open, and spittle drooled from her mouth. "Pep!" he moaned, barely aware that the two men were shouting at him. Jerry put his arms around the cat's neck and held her tightly against his chest. "You've killed her," he sobbed, as the men ran through the rocks and up to him. "You've killed her." Jerry buried his face in her warm fur, felt the quiver of her body, and wept heartbrokenly.

"Who in the name of the whole outdoors are you?" muttered one man, as he flung himself onto the rock, pulled Jerry violently by the shoulder, and sent him flying into the second man.

"It's all right, George," he said. "The cat's out like a light."

Held fast, Jerry pounded on the man's chest. "I hate you! I hate you! I hate you!" he sobbed. "You've killed Pepper!"

"Whoa." The man pinned Jerry's arms to his sides.

"Hold on, you little wildcat. George, help me hold him down."

"You had no right!" Jerry could barely see them through his blur of tears. "You've killed her." And at that be began to sob uncontrollably.

"Son," the man said gruffly, "I don't know where you came from, but you were mighty close to getting yourself killed just now. Why, a vicious animal like that could have torn you to pieces in seconds if my shot hadn't been true."

Jerry saw Pepper dimly through his tears, and she lay very still. "You had no right," he choked, but the men were busy looking at Pepper's red collar.

One of them whistled. "For crying out loud!" he said. "A collar!"

"It's against the law," Jerry said, shoving away the man who was holding him and falling back against the rocks. "You aren't supposed to hunt up here!" Now he was getting furiously angry.

The two men turned to him, frowning. "Son," one of them said, "we haven't killed that cougar. We shot her with the tranquilizing gun." Jerry snapped his mouth shut, stopping the angry words he had been ready to shout. "John and I have been up here for three weeks hunting mountain lion and tagging them."

Jerry gaped at them stupidly. He turned to Pepper. She

was breathing—he could see that now. "I—I don't understand."

The man knelt and put his hand on Jerry's shoulder. "Son, we're trying to save the cougars up here in the wild country. By tagging them we can keep track of how they come and go and see that they manage all right." He shook his head. "We aren't killing them!" And the emphatic way he spoke convinced Jerry completely.

"You mean Pepper's really all right?" The second man put something into Jerry's hand. It was a silver cylinder about two inches long, with an arrow tip and a red-tufted tail. "You shot her with this?" Jerry asked.

The man nodded. "We were on our way home and just happened to spot her up here on this rock. I didn't see her collar," he explained, then frowned and shook his head. "Even if I had I don't think it would have made much difference."

"She's my friend," Jerry said simply. "I've had her since she was a kit." He stroked Pepper gently. "Is she just asleep?"

"Yes, in a way. The drug puts them out for about an hour. We need that long to make all our tests. We weigh them, take measurements, and see if they are healthy. If not, we try to doctor them up. Then we tag them." He pulled a batch of yellow metal clips out of his pocket.

"We also tattoo them on the ear if we haven't caught

them before," said the other man. "By the way, my name's John Harrison. We work for the Wildlife Service. This is George Franklin."

Jerry took the big handkerchief that Mr. Harrison offered and wiped his eyes. Then he introduced himself. "I —I guess you must be wondering how—" Jerry rubbed the handkerchief across his nose. "You see the City Council gave us this notice," he started to explain. Quickly he told them why he had brought Pepper back to the mountains.

The men listened silently, then weighed his story. At last Mr. Harrison nodded. "I guess I'd have done the same thing if I'd been in your place," he said thoughtfully.

"That's right," said Mr. Franklin. "She's better off up here if she can hunt."

"But all day I've been trying to leave her," Jerry said. "Since she killed the sage hens, I know she can find food on her own." He sucked in his breath quickly as an idea came to him. "Do you think—"

Mr. Franklin sat back on his heels and smiled. "We were on our way back to the truck. It's parked down there." He pointed toward the canyon floor, but though Jerry squinted to see, it was hidden from his view.

"Would you help me?" he asked them.

They nodded. "We can take you up to the ranger station at Shuman's Peak, and you can call your parents from there and tell them you are on your way home."

Jerry nodded. "And Pepper?"

"Well," said Mr. Harrison gently, "we'll go ahead and tag her. Then if we should bag her again this winter we can keep in touch with you . . . let you know how she's making out. We get most of the same cats year after year. Some of them seem like old friends."

"It won't hurt her? To tag her?"

The man shook his head. "But we better get busy. We've spent about twenty minutes talking, and if you want to get away before she comes to, we haven't much time."

Jerry nodded and moved Pepper so her head rested in his lap. Mr. Harrison chuckled as the two men got right to work. "I never expected to see a youngster like you have a friend like this."

Jerry rubbed his cheek against Pepper's fur and brushed her softly. He held her head steady while a number was painstakingly tattooed inside the tip of her right ear. It was 352, a number that Jerry knew he would always remember. After they had clipped on the yellow ear tag with its bright streamers, he helped the men carry her into the protection of some rocks where she could rest safely until the effects of the narcotic wore off. It was a warm little den, and Jerry pulled some soft branches from a nearby bush and put them beneath her head.

"We'd best move out now," said Mr. Harrison, as he

looked at his watch. "She's due to be up and around in another ten or fifteen minutes."

Jerry nodded. He unbuckled Pepper's red collar, and he smoothed her fur down where the leather had ruffled it up. Then he backed out of the rocks and ran to join the men, who had picked up their guns and packs. It wasn't far to the truck. Jerry hadn't seen it before, because it was painted a dark government green that matched the pines. He climbed in next to the door and rolled down the window. The truck's engine ground over, then came to life with a chuff and sputter. It went into gear, and they started off.

"She'll be all right," Mr. Harrison said gently, as if he had read Jerry's mind.

But he couldn't help looking back, and he felt tears coming to his eyes. Then the truck turned, pines blotted out the rocky niche, and they picked up speed. "I'll write down my address and phone number," he said to the two men. "You'll let me hear about her?"

They turned to him. "Absolutely. We'll call you the minute we get in from each trek."

Jerry nodded. He still had Pepper's collar in his hand and fastened it through his jacket buttonhole carefully. He smiled. "She's really a silly old cat," he said affectionately. Then he stuck his head out the window and let the wind dry away the last of his tears.

Born in Nebraska and educated in California, Marian Rumsey is a travel enthusiast. She has lived aboard sailboats with her husband and two children for many years and they have gone some 70,000 miles at sea. They also have traveled by land in a camper-truck. Between these two modes of transportation, they move about twelve months a year and cannot call any one city or state their home.

The author has written many articles about the family cruises and is well known in boating and yachting circles. She also writes general travel articles in addition to her children's books.